# The Spell
# of the Occult

*An Exploration of the Mysterious and the Magical*

# The Spell
# of the Occult

*An Exploration of the Mysterious and the Magical*

## P.T. Joseph SJ

Jnana-Deepa Vidyapeeth (JDV)

2019

The Spell of the Occult: *An Exploration of the Mysterious and the Magical*: jointly published by the Rev. Dr. Ashish Amos of the Indian Society for Promoting Christian Knowledge (ISPCK), Post Box 1585, Kashmere Gate, Delhi-110006 and Jnana-Deepa Vidyapeeth, Pune, Maharashtra 411014.

© JDV, 2019

*Online order: http://ispck.org.in/book.php*

*Also available on amazon.in*

ISBN: 978-81-938241-6-0

*Cover picture credit: Internet sources*

*Laser typeset by*

**ISPCK,** Post Box 1585, 1654, Madarsa Road, Kashmere Gate, Delhi-110006 • *Tel:* 23866323

*e-mail:* ashish@ispck.org.in • ella@ispck.org.in
*website:* www.ispck.org.in

# Contents

# Preface

In our technological society, many people are under the spell of the occult. Today there is a tremendous fascination with the mysterious and the unknown and there is a boom in the occult, parapsychology, astrology and all the multitude of paraphernalia which surround them. It has turned into an enormous industry with a turnover of billions of dollars a year. The technological society not only entices people to react to the mystical and supernatural but also encourages and equips them to deal with them. The kingdom of the occult encompasses the globe like a spiderweb of immense proportions, its overall membership estimated in the hundreds of millions. The occult seduces the unwary with its offer of limited knowledge of the future and supposed control over the lives of others. It promises power.

In this context, 'The Spell of the Occult' by Dr. PT Joseph, S.J. exposes the reader to the many occult phenomena that we encounter in our societies. He also digs into the Biblical origins of the occult and gives a summary of occult and spiritual practices in the Catholic church. With his Scientific academic background, he delves into the possible scientific and psychological explanations of the occult. He demonstrates that the dividing line between spirituality and the occult can be very thin and therefore explores how 'discernment of spirits' is needed to distinguish between what is occult and what is genuine spirituality.

The first chapter of the book deals with proliferation of the occult in the modern society. It also critically looks at the scientific study of the occult through Parapsychology.

The second chapter exposes the reader to altered states of consciousness and its impact on occult phenomena. It also shows how healing is facilitated by the Placebo effect. Lunar effects on human mind and body and the power of emotions are also touched upon in this chapter.

The third chapter analyses the Bible from the perspective of the occult. On the one hand there is the condemnation of the occult practices in the Bible and on the other hand, occult practices were prevalent during Biblical times. Many a times, it is difficult to distinguish between the occult and the spiritual in the Bible.

The following chapter explores the place of supernatural in the Catholic Church and many popular practices are associated with the belief in the occult.

Chapter five deals with many occult practices and beliefs in the modern society. The next chapter tries to explain the place of occult in different world views.

The concluding chapter asserts that there is an urgent need for 'discernment of spirits' between the spiritual and the occult. The proliferation of the occult is a sign of the craving of the spiritual experience in our culture.

'The Spell of the Occult' challenges the reader to explore scientific and psychological explanation for the occult while at the same time connecting it with the spiritual dimension of the world. It is an attempt to bridge seemingly opposing world views of the occult and spiritual using scientific and psychological explanation. Anyone wanting to explore the occult phenomena will find this book to be enlightening.

The author, who is also my colleague and friend, is a versatile person with proven skill for research and writing. He has specialised in Physics, Theology and Management studies and contributed significantly in all these fields. I wish him all the best in his committed and creative study and research, especially in an area that is confusing, complex and bewildering.

*Dr. Kuruvilla Pandikattu, S.J.*
Dean, Faculty of Philosophy
Jnana-Deepa Vidyapeeth
Pune, India

# Chapter 1

# The Proliferation of the Occult

Occult is not a forgotten art. It is reappearing in the 21$^{st}$ century in various forms, sometimes in the guise of New Age Religions, modern scientific explanations and psychotherapies. When people get disenchanted with patriotism, social respectability, economic security, and even technological innovations, there seems very little within the established order of things that hold out any meaningfulness. A strong spiritual sense or meaning might have helped the situation. But today in many cases, religious beliefs are held purely on emotional or intellectual grounds and do not permeate life as a whole. The remedy to the meaninglessness of the present and the hopelessness of the future is being sought in experiments with unending sensual thrills - from alcohol and drugs to every form of sexual excesses, psychic séances, astrology, hypnotism and mediumship. Today there is a boom in the occult, parapsychology, astrology and all the multitude of paraphernalia which surround them. It has turned into an enormous industry with a turnover of billions of dollars a year. The technological society not only entices people to react to the mystical and supernatural but also encourages and equips them to deal with them.

Rapid advances in technology are transforming society in every way. Science does not seem to hold any absolute truths despite the many facilities it provides in terms of modern technologies. Even the discipline of Physics whose laws once went unchallenged had to submit to uncertainty in terms of the nature of fundamental particles, the string theory, the nature of vacuum where electrons and positrons are created out of nothing, the limitless expansion of the universe, etc. Of late, we seem to have grown through the confident adolescence of science into a philosophical maturity, and we are prepared not only to admit our own ignorance, but to grapple with the fact that there are some things we can never know. Armed with the principle of quantum mechanics and a host of other hidden factors, we appear to be better equipped than ever before to break through some of the misty fringes of the unknown.

Of late, we appear to have come through the certain youthfulness of science into a philosophical maturity, and we are ready to concede our own obliviousness and to grapple with the ambiguity that there are a few things we can never know. Having been confronted with our own vulnerability and a large group of other concealed factors, we appear to be prepared to travel through the dim edges of the obscure.

The occult has a very long history. Its theories and practices involving knowledge or use of supernatural forces or beings have occurred in all human societies throughout recorded history. It should be granted that there were considerable variations both in their nature and in the attitude of societies toward the occult practices. Those aspects of occultism that appear to be common to all human societies are divination, magic, witchcraft, and foretelling of the future. Humanity appears to have an ever-present need to be engaged and excited by the supernatural, and this is indicated by the fact that topics like magic, prophecies of the future, ghosts and the occult have a continuous tradition in literature. Ranging from the earliest examples such as the Gilgamesh epic, they come up in the works of every age and every culture like medieval romances, the Renaissance plays of Shakespeare or the vampire novels of the 21st century. In the twenty-first century, monsters, magic, and the occult tend to be common themes in movie theaters, video games, and children's books. Occult practices such as freemasonry, luciferianism, the Illuminati, or just blatant witchcraft and satanic sorcery are obscure but looked upon with awe in some circles. There is always a next degree to attain, a new order to join, and a deeper understanding to learn. Many people claim a sixth sense or subtle perception ability to perceive the unseen world of angels, ghosts, spirits and auras.

There are many esoteric groups that dabble in issues related to the spirit world ranging from astrology, mediumship, witchcraft, to the invocation of spirit-guides. Across the ages, humans tried to connect and engage with other life- forms in the higher realms. It is an age old pursuit but with immense following in today's world and often commanding more fascination and allegiance than the wisdom of official religious or spiritual practices.

One of the famous occult experiences in the ancient world was the Oracles of Delphi in Greece. Dating back to 1400 BC. The Oracle of Delphi was the most famous shrine in all Greece. Built around a sacred spring, Delphi was considered to be the center of the world by the Greeks. People came from all over Greece and beyond to have their questions about future answered by the Pythia, the priestess of Apollo. And her answers, usually mysterious, could determine the course of everything from when a farmer planted his seedlings, to when an empire declared war. The priestess was a woman over fifty years of age, lived apart from her husband, and dressed in a maiden's clothes. The legend is that the Pythia first enters the inner chamber of the temple. Then, she sits on a tripod and inhales the light hydrocarbon gasses that escape from a chasm on the porous earth. After falling into a trance, she listens to the questions of the people who come to consult her. Then she mutters words incomprehensible to ordinary people. These words are then interpreted by the priests of the sanctuary in a common language and delivered to those who had requested them. Nevertheless, the oracles were always open to interpretation and often signified dual and opposing meanings. The Oracles of Delphi determined the fate of many nations and large number of people consulted Pythia.

Nowadays, in some places it is fashion to accept anything that is baffling as authentic. People quote the statement of a clairvoyant about their past incarnations or the state of their auras as positive proof of supernatural. There are lots of people who go to psychics and astrologers. Some people have special gifts or charisms. It is certain that human beings possess latent powers of which they are only dimly aware, and that these latent powers produce a variety of phenomena, from poltergeist activity to clairvoyance. An illustration can be found in the autobiography of the 'clairvoyant' Pieter van der Hurk, better known as Peter Hurkos.[1] In 1943, Hurkos was working as a house painter when he fell from a ladder and fractured his skull. When he woke up in the hospital, he discovered that he possessed the gift of second sight. He knew things about his fellow patients without being told. The chief drawback of this unusual power was that he was no longer able to return to his old job as a painter; he had lost the faculty of concentration. His mind was like a radio set picking up too many stations. From the social point of view, he was useless until he conceived the idea of using his peculiar powers on the stage. He was more successful foretelling the future or solving a murder case by handling a garment of the victim, and such other clairvoyant activities. The capacity to enjoy 'subtle vibrations' is an important part of our energy outlets. The definition of a living organism is an organism capable of responding to energy vibrations. These vibrations constitute 'meanings.' Whether I am relaxing in front of a fire, or enjoying a beautiful sunset, or responding to a symphony, I am registering meanings and recording vibrations.

Interest in the psychic sciences and in matters strange and sensational became widespread during the 1970s. Psychic healers made extravagant claims. People were fascinated with spiritualism. Many witches came out of the closet. But the greatest barometer of the occult explosion was the mushrooming interest in divination—that is, discerning the future. Tarot, I Ching, palmistry, and Ouija boards were used by many people, along with astrology. Many institutions of higher learning, including prestigious universities, began to offer courses on aspects of the occult. Universities instituted sponsored research on parapsychological phenomena.[2]

In this period of uncertainty and restlessness, people are turning more than ever to spirituality, seeking security and meaningfulness in life. The scientific and social upheavals have been unleashing a new religious search. And part of this spiritual search has been in the area of the occult, the paranormal and the psychical. This search is well described in this quotation from a cover story in the Time Magazine:

A wave of fascination with the occult is noticeable throughout the country. It first became apparent a few years ago in the astrology boom which continues. But today it also extends all the way from Satanism and witchcraft to the edges of science as in Astronaut Edger Mitchell's experiment in extrasensory perception from abroad Apollo 14. In this field, serious researchers of parapsychology are increasingly interacting with devotees of such claimed occult gifts as prophecy and telepathy to probe the powers of the human mind.[3]

The reappearance of the occult in the seventies was not limited to North America. It was a worldwide phenomenon. It never declined in much of Asia and Africa, and Europe also witnessed an increased interest in the occult.[4] Furthermore, the occult did not decline after the seventies. Rather, it travelled down a different path as part of the New Age movements self-improvement groups and various worldviews found in the postmodern world.

## Harry Potter and the Occult

On 30th June 1997, thousands of copies of the first Harry Potter book filled the shelves of bookstores in the U. K.[5] Since then, over 450 million copies of Harry Potter books have been sold worldwide and the eight Harry Potter movies have raked in $7.7 billion at the box office worldwide.[6] In 1997, kids became crazy over the first Harry Potter books, wanting to read what their friends told them were "good" books. Parents watched their kids reading the thick volumes and were glad to see the children doing something they thought of as "more productive" and "educational" than just playing video games or watching TV.

Untold millions of young people were being taught to think, speak, dress and act like witches by filling their heads with the contents of these books. The first book of the series, entitled "Harry Potter and the Sorcerer's Stone," finds the orphan, Harry Potter, embarking upon a new realm where he is taken to "Hogwart's School of Witchcraft and Wizardry." At this occult school, Harry Potter learns how to obtain and use witchcraft equipment. Harry also learns a new vocabulary, including words such as "Azkaban", "Circe", "Draco", "Erised", "Hermes", and "Slytherin," all of which are names of real devils or demons.

*Harry Potter* created in children an interest in the occult. J.K. Rowling portrays characters who mostly are witches and wizards, and they are superior to non-magic people. In addition to those already mentioned above, other real occult practices in the books are the Runes, numerology, and crystal gazing. The books also refer to alchemy, amulets, charms, contact with the dead, the Dark Side, and many other occult practices or concepts. Using "good" magic to fight "bad" magic is a major component of the plot.

Harry Potter is well known for his thunderbolt scar on his forehead. The scar is described as "a curiously shaped cut, like a bolt of lightning."[7] As Harry grows older, he eventually learns that the scar on his forehead came as the result of a powerful evil curse from the evil dark wizard, Voldemort.[8] The startling thing about the thunderbolt is that it is often used in occult imagery, especially in Satanism. Anton Szandor Lavey, the founder of the *Church of Satan*, often wore a medallion of an inverted pentagram with a thunderbolt through the centre of it. Thunderbolts also appeared as the SS symbol of Hitler's Special Forces. In the *Philosopher's Stone* Harry becomes fascinated by images of his dead parents in the *Mirror of Erised* in Chapter 1. `Erised' is the word `desire' spelled backwards, and those who investigate the mirror are meant to see their uttermost desires. In occultism, mirrors are commonly used for divination. This technique is called "Scrying."

The general message that the Harry Potter books convey is that 'witchcraft is fun'. You can get what you want, control others, and look cool in the meantime. Children were being subtly indoctrinated into occultism, and they were being encouraged to encounter powerful, manipulative, evil forces. Those children are adults now and its impact is very strong in our world today.

## Popular Occult Themes

The 31$^{st}$ of October is known as *Halloween in the US*. This holiday was relatively obscure till late 19th century in America. It was brought to USA by Irish and Scottish immigrants. People had been carving gourds and pumpkins and been using them as lanterns long before the practice was associated with Halloween. The origin of Halloween is Celtic in tradition, and having to do with observing the end of summer by sacrifices to gods in Druidic tradition. In what is now Britain and France, it was the beginning of the Celtic year, and they believed Samhain, the lord of death, would send evil spirits abroad to attack humans, who could escape only by assuming disguises and looking like evil spirits themselves. The waning of the sunlight and the approach of dark winter made the evil spirits rejoice and play nasty tricks. It is also a time they believed that the veil between the living and the dead is the thinnest, and so it is an opportune time for them to contact the dead.

Ghosts have been around forever. Paranormal reality TV shows were a new breed of activity in the US. Reality TV made its mark on the avocation of ghost hunting. Thanks to these shows, ghost hunting has gathered interest around the world. Televisions have been showing paranormal experiences of telepathy, clairvoyance and telekinesis, and thus popularizing the belief in the occult. 'Paratainment' events, such as group ghost hunts, paranormal conferences, and ghost tours are blossoming in many parts of the world.

## The Sixth Sense

We perceive the world through the five physical senses (i.e. smell, taste, sight, touch and sound) connected to our mind and feelings. In the normal state we know and understand the external world through and by the senses. The eye reveals to us the beauties of light, and by its aid the wondrous diversities of nature. The ear brings to the mind the varied sounds, makes oral speech and the sweet harmonies of music possible. In the same way, the other senses also help us to live fully. Ordinarily we rely on these senses as our guides, and so complete is our reliance that we recognize no other avenue to knowledge of the external world; yet at times we find that our minds extend beyond the senses and have capabilities which cannot be referred to them. There is an interior perception, which has been called the sixth sense. Sixth sense is our ability to perceive the subtle-dimension or the unseen world of angels, ghosts, vibrations etc. It also includes our ability to understand the subtle cause and effect relationship behind many events, which is beyond the understanding of the intellect. Extrasensory perception (ESP), clairvoyance, premonition, intuition are synonymous with the sixth sense or subtle perception ability. Many people seem to possess this ability of the sixth sense especially in times of danger and emergencies.

## *The Modern Use of Occult Symbols*

All of us encounter logos on household items, on cars, in TV ads, on billboards, on newspapers, on magazines, on insignias, all over sporting events and on branded clothes. Logos are one of the results of extensive studies in cognitive sciences, neuropsychology and biology. Those studies constitute the core of marketing, a heavily funded field which keeps its findings totally secret from the general public. The huge visibility of corporate logos is an opportunity for the elite to showcase their beliefs and their power. The same way occult symbols are inserted on buildings and sites , they are hidden in plain view on corporate logos. Throughout history, symbols have been used to convey hidden spiritual messages, which often have double or multiple meanings. The trademark, brand name or celebrity figure serves as a sort of shorthand for the values consumers associate with particular goods and services. Once learned and associated, the symbol's identity and the emotions it elicits become ingrained in the mind forever, affecting our subunconscious mind to think of thoughts connected with the symbol. The effectiveness of these symbols depends on an understanding of Carl Jung's theory of the "collective unconscious". This idea, in brief, posits that humans have a genetic memory of ancient memories of humanity; a remembrance of the same rites of passages, ideas, images, etc. He calls these embedded symbols "archetypes", and they are a part of our makeup. According to Jung, we know them not from personal experience but from the thousands of years of experience from our ancestors. Recurring symbols include the dot in circle, Eye of Horus, rising sun, compass and square, 666, two towers, Star of David, pentagrams and pyramid without a capstone. Symbols and iconography from modern and ancient religions, paganism, the occult and astrology are being fed to us, via the media on a daily basis. And we are entirely unaware of it. The power of magic works very much along the same lines as artistic works. One difference is that the occultist intentionally creates scenarios in which they make themselves susceptible to forces of influence. The use of intricate symbols and archetypes during ritual and meditation bypasses the iron doorways of the rational and critical mind to gain entry into the subconscious. Through a form of self-suggestion and deliberate programming, the magician can create change in their interior and exterior environment. Logos with hidden messages are designed to target our minds, specially the subconscious mind as our mind controls what we actually do in actions. The advertisers use these hidden messages to condition our minds and once it did so, it can control our thought patterns to a certain degree without our knowledge. Corporations and the governments are obsessed with subliminal messages because they are effective at manipulating our thought patterns at the subconscious level. Here are few of the symbols and their associated occult messages. These subliminal messages may have nothing to do with the genuine logo makers or the concerned organizations. Perhaps it can be utterly coincidental or it might be intentional.

*Fig. 1: The MercedesBenz Logo*

A person looking at the Mercedes Benz logo above may associate it with luxury, style, class, and comfort. This may be what it means today, but for thousands of years that logo had a vey different meaning. It was the "Triquetra" of the Druids and Celtics, who used its great secret. The symbol's natural shape has the ability to stimulate the human psyche and awaken spiritual powers within us when we look upon it. The Triquetra was principally a ceremonial device in Neolithic Europe, used in magic, ritual and religious incantation. Superimposing the Triquetra over the Mercedes logo immediately produces a very obvious parallel.

### 666

Six hundred and sixty-six is called the "number of the Beast" in chapter 13 of the Book of Revelation.[9] The 666 symbolism is hidden is many corporate logos. Many logos have made use of this number as in the google chrome symbol, Olympics symbol, Vodafone symbol, etc. Google chrome search engine symbol–dot in circle exhibits the subliminal satanic devil number 666. Dot in circle is also a sexual symbol.

*Fig. 2: Google Chrome Search Engine Symbol*

## The Winged Sun-Disk Symbol

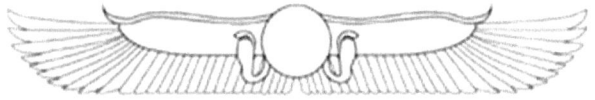

*Fig. 3: The Winged Sun-Disk Symbol*

The winged sun-disk symbol is an ancient Egyptian symbol, which traditionally depicted two serpents on the wings, representing the goddesses that protected Upper and Lower Egypt. The winged sun is still being used today by groups like the Freemasons, the Theosophists and the Rosicrucians. The winged sun-disk symbol, which has become a recognizable logo in the automotive industry and is used in the Bentley, Mini, Harley Davidson, Chrysler, Aston Martin and Chevrolet logos.

## The Vesica Piscis

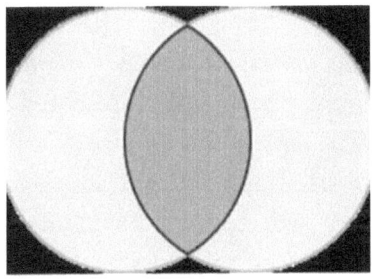

*Fig. 4: The Vesica Piscis*

Another prominent modern corporate logo that has ancient mystical and magical meanings is the Vesica Piscis, an ancient symbol that is the shape of two interlocking circles and is part, of sacred geometry. It is widely agreed that it represents the female principle, "the vulva of the Goddess." In modern culture, this ancient symbol that has 'sexual' associations is used as the basis of the logos for several leading fashion brands, namely Channel, Gucci and DC Shoes. The symbol is even the logo for Mastercard.

## The Pentagram

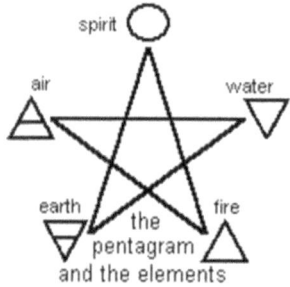

*Fig. 5: The Pentagram Symbol*

The pentagram, or five-pointed star, has been in existence for thousands of years. Over that time, it has had many meanings, uses, and depictions associated with it. Up until medieval times, the five points of the pentagram represented the five wounds of Christ on the Cross. It was a symbol of Christ the Saviour. Pentagrams were used symbolically in ancient Greece and Babylonia, and are used today as a symbol of faith by many Wiccans, akin to the use of the cross by Christians and the Star of David by the Jews. The pentagram has magical associations. Many people who practice Neo-pagan faiths wear jewellery incorporating the symbol. It is considered a sacred symbol because the number five is considered a mystical number. We see five over and over in nature. An Inverted Pentagram is used by Satanists to represent the Satan of the Bible.

## Snakes and Dragons

These largely feared creatures have long been used to symbolise the cold-blooded and callous ruling 'elite'. From ancient myths like St.George and the Dragon to more modern portrayals encompassing corporate identities and Hollywood blockbusters, lizard-like beasts play a significant role in illuminati imagery. This is partly due to the fact that the emotionless business houses relate closely to the characteristics these creatures have always been revered for. yet the symbolism of the snake may also be linked to the controversial theory that these archaic interbreeding bloodlines.

Why major modern corporations choose to incorporate these ancient logos from occult societies has been associated with the fact that such symbols are, "magically charged to focus the subconscious to perform particular tasks." In other words, these logos are much more powerful than we may think. Setting the question of magic aside, these logos offer a great deal of insight into the belief systems – both superstitious and spiritual – of the individuals that created them.

## All Seeing Eye

The All-Seeing Eye symbol is as a part of the design of the Great Seal of the United States of America, which appears on the US dollar bill. Set within a triangle, a single eye is surrounded by rays of light and its symbolic meaning is God watching over humankind. The eye itself is a powerful and popular symbol, and the All-Seeing Eye has its roots in the Egyptian Eye of Horus. The fact that the Great Seal was a symbol that belonged to Freemasonry and alchemy prior to its adoption as part of the Great Seal of the USA has given rise to many conspiracy theories. That the All-Seeing Eye is also the symbol of the Illuminati and Freemasonry which are secretive organizations.

## Baphomet

The Baphomet is a winged goat with a masculine torso and breasts. He has a blazing torch between his horns, and cloven feet. Adding to the confusion, one arm is male, and the other is female. The image made its first appearance in Eliphas

Levi's Dogma and Rituals of High Magic(1854). The picture influenced illustrations of the Devil, not only in Tarot card illustrations but also among latter-day rock bands and, among Satanists. Baphomet was first described at the trials of the Knights Templar, centuries before Levi's interpretation.

## Occult Jewellery and Pendants

Unknowingly many young people are wearing jewellery and pendants without knowing their connection with Satanic worship. Some examples are the following;

*The Pentagram:* The traditional five-pointed star, most often shown within a circle.

Goat's Head within a Pentagram: *The sigil of Baphomet,*

*Number 666:* The number of the beast in the Book of Revelation, considered by many Christians to represent Satan.

*Upside-Down Cross:* A mockery of Jesus' death on the cross. Sometimes the cross is shown with broken "arms."

*Upside-Down Cross Incorporating an Inverted Question Mark:* The cross of confusion, questioning the authority and power of Jesus.

*Quarter Moon and Star:* Represents the Moon Goddess Diana and Lucifer.

*Inverted Swastika:* The swastika is another once-honorable symbol that simply represented the perpetual progression of the four seasons, the four winds, the four elements, and so forth. Occultists are said to invert it to show the elements of nature turned against themselves and out of harmony with God's divine plan of balance.

## Witchcraft

The perceptions of people have been changing about Witchcraft. From J.K. Rowling's Harry Potter books to self-described witches agitating for social parity with mainstream religions, there are lots of signs to recognize its growth. In an age of science and scepticism, it may be difficult to understand why intelligent people would be drawn to witchcraft. It encompasses both a methodology of casting spells and invoking spirits and an ideology that encourages finding divinity in nature and people.

People all over the world have been practising witchcraft for centuries, and is emerging once more from the shadows as an answer to scepticism and materialism leading to an alternate spirituality. In some cases, witches do not directly worship Satan or practice Satanism. Historically the witchcraft label has been applied to practices people believe influence the mind, body or property of others against their will, or to practices that the person doing the labelling believes undermine the social or religious order. The concept of magicians influencing other people's body or property against their will was clearly present in many cultures, as traditions in both folk magic and religious magic have the purpose of countering malicious magic or identifying malicious magic users. It is believed in many cultures that malicious magic users can become a credible cause of disease, sickness in animals, bad luck, sudden death, impotence and other misfortunes. Black magic can be defined as belief of supernatural practices used to harm, kill, or cause misfortune to others. Because these supernatural forces are thought to govern the course of natural events, control of these forces gives humans control over nature. And hence a human can use un-natural forces i.e. Black magic. People believe in Evil spells which are verbal formulae believed to have magical force. Very often, the effectiveness of black magic depends on the belief system of the victim.

*Wicca* is the name given to a subset of witchcraft by its founder Gerald Gardner in the 1950s. Because witchcraft is often defined as a methodology and Wicca as an ideology, a person who considers himself a witch but not a Wiccan may participate in many of the same practices as a Wiccan, such as casting spells, divining the future, perhaps even banding together with others to form a coven.

Occult practices seem to have the capacity to satisfy daily needs of people who want to control their destinies. Self-help literature helped them to take steps toward improved prosperity, health, and happiness in their daily situations. Psychics offered physical healing and spiritual advice on how to deal with everyday problems. People thought that by knowing the future they could change it, take the steps necessary to avoid harm, or restore balance to life. Communicating with a dead relative may seem to offer consolation and connectivity. Renewed health and good fortune could come from the practice of knowing the future. People believed that engaging in occult activities was a way to improve their life situations.

Witchcraft seduces the ignorant with its offer of limited knowledge of the future and supposed control over the lives of others. It promises power. If someone involved in the occult can provide secret information to an individual that only the witch knows, and then predict something that does indeed occur, then the witch has secured power over the other person through fear. Witches offer a small degree of certainty in a world of uncertainty. Moving outside the realm of established religion, it promises things that the Church forbids. It provides a sense of belonging, so desperately needed by people who reject God's love. At its heart it is egocentric. Witches are seeking first their own ends and then the ends of others. It provides no exit from the realities of life and the problems of life but is merely a diversion.

## Understanding the Occult

What is the occult? According to the *Oxford English Dictionary*, the term *occult* was first used in 1545, meaning that which is "not apprehended, or not apprehensible by the mind; beyond the range of understanding or of ordinary knowledge." Over the years, the word received an additional meaning, denoting the knowledge or use of agencies of a secret and mysterious nature such as magic, alchemy, astrology, and theology[10]. Modern definitions contain similar ideas such as knowledge which is mysterious or knowledge beyond the range of ordinary knowledge or a secret which is disclosed to the initiated or the occult pertains to magic, astrology, and other alleged sciences claiming use or knowledge of the secret, mysterious or supernatural.[11]

What is our reaction when we hear tales of haunted houses, accounts of telepathy, materialization of ectoplasm, clairvoyance, mediums contacting the dead, the various forms of divination, mystic experiences, trance and rapture, hypnotism, the survival of bodily death, possession, etc.? On the one hand, occult phenomena should be carefully investigated for the sake of obtaining knowledge, but on the other hand, it should be investigated for the sake of unmasking charlatans. We know that the occult phenomena exercised a profound influence on the ancient civilisations and that some of the noblest men of all races were inspired by them and regarded them with reverence and awe. Are the phenomena we call 'occult' merely attract and enthral crowds or are there spiritual influences such as raised consciousness leading to a deeper understanding of the supernatural? Occult phenomena are hidden in their nature, not amenable to ordinary scientific methods of investigation with instruments of precision, and legitimately form the field of investigation of occult science. Occult science has two enemies to contend with -the sceptical materialist who denies everything, and the credulous charlatan who believes everything. Serious researchers need to find the middle way between these two extremes; they must, on the one hand, avoid credulity, and on the other, recognise that the nature of proof available concerning the occult realms differs from that available for natural sciences. Our world today is engulfed in a kind of spiritual schizophrenia, based on a dualistic set of perceptions whereby we divide reality into the opposing categories of God versus humankind, spirit versus matter, the sacred versus the secular.

What is the relationship of the occult to science? Prior to the seventeenth century, science and the occult maintained a close relationship. However, with the rise of modern science, the occult was perceived as having more magical qualities. In the last half of the twentieth century, another change took place. Investigators began to apply scientific methods to occult phenomena. And this field of investigation became the field of Parapsychology. Parapsychology has to some extent achieved a degree of scientific legitimacy.[12]

How does the occult relate to religion? Occult is best seen as a quasi-religious development. The occult comes in two related forms. It includes certain occult practices—that is, the occult arts such as divination, fortune-telling, spiritism, magic, and so on. There is also an occult worldview. Though the practice of the occult arts presupposes an occult worldview, this aspect of the occult tends to be more magical. Yet even the occult arts have religious aspects; they attempt to provide meaning, contacts with the sacred, and at times, a basis for community.[13] However, the occult's clearest religious expression is in its worldview.

Prior to the seventeenth century, most people in society embraced one or the other aspects of the occult. Then the eighteenth century, the Age of Reason, dealt a blow to the occult worldview. As with any religious movement, the occult has its peaks and valleys. Apparently, what surfaced in the 1970s was a peak of popular interest in the occult. This caused a renewed interest in certain occult practices such as astrology cartomancy, crystal-gazing, palmistry, Ouija boards, prophetic dreams and visions, psychometry, numerology, I Ching, witchcraft, Satanism, spiritualism, magic and paranormal experiences.

Ron Enroth says that collectively these occult phenomena have laid claim to the following distinctive characteristics. One, they disclose and communicate information unavailable to humans through normal means, that is, the five senses. Two, they place persons in contact with untapped powers and paranormal energies. Three, they facilitate the acquisition and mastery of power in order to manipulate or influence other people into certain actions.[14]

Occult activities are practiced by individuals and groups. The occult lends itself to private activity, and this may be where most of the action takes place. Though there exist occult organizations which provide fellowship and community, they are not central to them. Occult is an invisible religion because it is private, personal, and not regularly institutionalized or monitored by priests or contained in organizations. Thus, it cannot be mapped. And if community is not central, symbols and sacramental objects are.[15] Performing the correct procedures is vital to obtaining results in the occult.

But not all occult activities are without an organizational structure. There exist groups in which occult practices are so central that scholars have classified them as occult bodies. Some examples include witch covens, Satanist groups, Theosophical societies, Rosicrucian orders, Swedenborgianism, and a vast array of Spiritualist bodies.

## A Spiritual Thirst

The early occult explosion—from the late sixties to the mid-seventies of the last century—was closely related to the counterculture and the use of psychedelic drugs, and it was largely a youth phenomenon. The most prominent tendency in this part of the occult explosion was a dabbling in occult practices, especially astrology and divination. In fact, to many the occult was something of a pop religion, a fad of the youth culture, a means to proclaim the new Aquarian Age. However, as the more radical counter cultural context disappeared, the occult arts mostly receded from public view, while many occult groups lived on as isolated cults or attained a respectable presence in society.[16]

Why did this so-called occult-explosion occur in the late twentieth century? Interest in the occult has grown significantly in periods of rapid social breakdown, when establishments cease to provide readily accepted answers and people turn elsewhere for assurance. That is one reason for the occult explosion. The twentieth century was congenial to occult developments, including Transcendentalism, Spiritualism, the Shakers, Theosophy, New Thought, Christian Science, and many Eastern faiths.

The occult's insistence that experience is the path to knowledge and enlightenment also had its parallel in the larger society. The cognitive processes had been dethroned, and experience was the new king. The many religious therapies associated with the human potential and New Age movements closely resembled their secular counterparts. By the late-twentieth century, scientific and secular forces had drastically diminished a sense of the supernatural, the transcendent and the sacred. Because of their worldview and desire to validate their activities, many occultists rejected a concept of the supernatural. Nevertheless, they engaged themselves in a quest for other aspects of the transcendent, whether they are the forces of nature or of the hidden depths of the mind. Occultism, with its long history of unorthodox beliefs and practices, is above all a declaration of the existence of powers emanating from beyond. Thus, it is a counter-religion in quest of aspects of transcendence that lie outside the Judeo-Christian tradition. Occult movements met a deep spiritual thirst, and this is a major part of their attraction today.

We ought to approach the occult arts in the same spirit in which we approach any other phenomena. They are not supernatural, they break no natural laws; they are rare and little understood. As soon as we understand their rationale, they cease to be supernatural and become natural.

## Occult Terms: Meaning

| Aquarian Age | Age of Aquarius is an astrological term denoting the current astrological age, depending on the method of calculation but usually beginning from 11th November of 2011. |
|---|---|
| Astrology, Horoscopes | This is offered as a means for the stars and planetary systems to guide the subject |

| Aura | these are colored light emanations that surround people. Some claim special power to see these auras and claim to interpret moods and personal characteristics by defining the colours of light |
|---|---|
| Automatic Writing | authors claim to have contact with spirits that take over their bodies and write through them. This is a form of mediumship. |
| Clairaudience | The practice of hearing audible voices that other people do not naturally hear |
| Clairvoyance | This is the practice of seeing things that other people do not naturally see. Usually this comes through dreams, visions, or precognition. Crystals and Coloured Stones. As with occult practitioners, New Agers often believe that energy or vibration qualities exist in certain stones and crystals. These are used for a variety of rituals, including physical healing and meditation. |
| Crop Circle | A crop circle is a pattern created by flattening a crop, usually a cereal and is seen especially in England. |
| Divination | This is any means of predicting an unknown event with the aid of physical objects or events that are read or interpreted, such as tarot cards, runes, crystal gazing, omens, scrying, palmistry, and dreams. |
| Ectoplasm | It is a term used in spiritualism to denote a substance or spiritual energy exteriorized by physical mediums |
| Extrasensory Perception (ESP) | The occult experimentation with ESP existed prior to the New Age era. ESP is used by "gifted" New Agers who claim the ability to know things through premonitions that are not common to other people. |
| Host hunter | A **ghost hunter** is a person who engages in ghost hunting or the process of investigating locations that are allegedly haunted |
| Medium | A person who acts as a conduit for communication between the spirits and humanity through a variety of manifestations. |
| New Age Religions | New Age is a term applied to a range of spiritual or religious beliefs and practices that developed in Western nations during the 1970s |
| Numerology | New Agers mimic the occult with numerology by affixing values and meanings to certain numbers in order to interpret them as meaningful signs for past or future events. |

| Out-of-Body Experiences | While the body is at rest, the ability of a person to move out-of-body and travel. It is also called astral projection. |
| Psychic | A person who acts as a medium and who uses auras, numerology, divination, clairvoyance, clairaudience, oracles, telepathy, or ESP as a means for communicating unknown information to the participant. |
| Psychokinesis and Telekinesis | In the occult, psychokinesis is the belief that gifted people can move physical objects by use of their mental powers. New Agers believe that these powers belong to gifted people. |
| Séance | A session with a medium before one or more people, in which the medium attempts contact with deceased humans, angels, or other spirit-beings, usually directed toward contact with a specific departed person known by the participant |
| Telepathy | adherents sometimes claim telepathy as a medium for communication with the living or dead. It is said to be nonverbal communication directly from one mind to another. |
| Telekinesis | Telekinesis or Psychokinesis is an alleged psychic ability allowing a person to influence a physical system or object without physical interaction. |

## Scientific Study of the Occult: Parapsychology

In our materialistic and technological society, it is difficult to take the paranormal seriously. Can my thoughts be transferred to another person at a distance without any information being exchanged? Does telepathy really occur? Can a person's mind influence the external material world without exerting any muscular or mechanical action? That is, can psycho-kinesis really take place? As far as we know, there is no known mechanism to explain such incidents. Performing psychics, metal benders, healers, fortune tellers, ghost hunters, medium, clairvoyants, diviners, crop-circle fanatics etc. are included in the field of parapsychology.

Para-psychology can be defined as the attempt to apply scientific method or critical investigation to phenomena which are 'paranormal.' 'Paranormal' here means whatever is outside the normal paradigm of science and critical reasoning. Paradigm means a set of generally accepted assumptions and rules regarding the nature of the problems in each discipline and the appropriate means of addressing them. Paradigms are like windows through which we see reality. Paradigms are very important because they usually decide what we can observe.

What Para-psychology studies are often called 'Psi' (A Greek letter usually used to denote the unknown). This is the general term for extrasensory perception (ESP) and extrasensory motor ability. Extrasensory here means not necessarily beyond all our senses but beyond their known activities or outside our present paradigms. Also, the term does not necessarily mean "spiritual". Psi is a general term that includes a wide variety of human experiences having the common characteristics that, in terms of the contemporary understanding of a physical world, they cannot have happened. Psi includes the three well studied forms of extrasensory perception: telepathy, clairvoyance and precognition. In our cotemporary picture of the physical world, there can be no telepathy (mind to mind contact over a distance), because there is no known physical energy to carry the information. The idea of clairvoyance, which, for example, enables a person to identify cards in the middle of a pack of shuffled cards successfully without looking at them, makes no sense either, because all the light energy that would provide information about the patterns on the card is screened from the person. Precognition – knowledge of the future before it happens – similarly makes no sense in terms of widely accepted physics because the future does not yet exist.

Psi also includes psycho-kinesis, which is the ability to produce physical effects on objects by simply wishing for them to take on such and such a condition. Experimental subjects try to influence the fall of dice that are thrown by a machine or the internal electronic circuitry of a machine that they do not understand in the least and sometimes they are successful. But contemporary physics provides no explanation of how the action is performed. Psi may be the mechanism behind many other exotic phenomena, such as the experience of consciousness leaving the body (Out of Body Experiences), of healing when no healing can be expected, of a person surviving physical death and communicating through medium. Even more exotic reports of experiences such as floating in the air, magic and witchcraft may fall under the Psi label. The category of uncanny, seemingly impossible things that could be termed as Psi phenomenon is very large. Paranormal phenomena go beyond the known laws of cause and effect. They refer to perception without mediation of the known sensory or to movement without participation directly or indirectly of known motor process.

## History of Parapsychology

With the Age of Enlightenment, a large-scale socio-cultural transformation process began, which can be concisely characterized by a triad of individualization, secularization and scientific exploration. Consequently, secular, rational and scientific concepts superseded religions' grasp on social life, and the monopoly of religion as a genuine compass for social values and epistemological frameworks. Morally and socially acceptable behaviour was substituted by a plurality of scientific concepts and secularized philosophical systems. One of the first social scientists, who reflected on the complex cultural process of secularization, was Max Weber, who coined the well-known phrase "disenchantment of the world."[17] Accordingly, religious and spiritual affairs have not been fully abandoned from the cultural charter of modem societies but rather been relegated to the status of private matters. The interpretational framework for dealing with exceptional or anomalous experiences has certainly changed over the last two hundred years, they have been considered suspicious, at best, if not outright pathological, within the framework of orthodox clinical psychology and psychiatry. It mainly was parapsychology and, a century later, predominantly transpersonal psychology that have dealt with exceptional experiences by emphasizing their inherent potential for human growth and personal development.

Parapsychology from its early days, and in a way like that of experimental psychology, had geared to empiricism. Correspondingly, it was mainly interested in experimentally exploring and explaining the *extraordinary* phenomena within the framework of a verifiable scientific theory. Consequently, parapsychology has mainly focused on tracking down a presumptive clandestine mechanism that was later labelled Psi and assumed to be something along the lines of a physical science. It is worth noting that, in the course of time, the concept underlying Psi was gradually decontextualized from spiritual or metaphysical beliefs.

According to the Parapsychological Association, the definition of parapsychology is, "the scientific and scholarly study of certain unusual events associated with human experience,"[18] which fall into the following three categories, extrasensory perception (ESP), psycho-kinesis (PK) and phenomena suggestive of survival after bodily death, including near-death experiences, apparitions, and reincarnation.

Like all other sciences, parapsychology has gone through identifiable phases of development.

1.  The era before 1882 is considered as being the pre-scientific period.

2.  From 1882 to 1930 is considered as the early scientific period.

3.  From 1930-1970 is considered as the mid-scientific period.

4.  From 1970- till date is considered as the scientific period.

During the pre-scientific period, Franz Anton Mesmer came on the scene with his demonstrations of what was known as mesmerism, which may be equated to both hypnosis and animal magnetism. He attempted to evoke an interest in the paranormal but his efforts were effectively suppressed in 1784 by the French Academy of Sciences. Interest in the manifestations of mesmerism remained dormant, finding some expression in the newly emerging spiritualist movement, with interest in mediumistic experiences.

Interest in the scientific study of psychical phenomena began with a movement known as *spiritism* or *spiritualism* in New York in 1848 with the well-known case of Fox Sisters: Kate, Margaretta, and Leah. They claimed to hear strange rapping noises in their bedroom. They convinced a few people that they were getting messages from spirits. They went on tour performing séances, which became popular both in the U.S. and Europe. In the 19th century, several eminent scientists, including biologist Alfred Russell Wallace and chemist Sir William Crookes, became interested in spirit communication. In 1888, the sisters confessed that they had produced the raps by cracking their toe-joints and that they made bumping noises by fastening an apple to a string under their petticoats and surreptitiously bouncing it off the floor. In 1853, physicist Michael Faraday did his own experiments on table tilting and concluded that the phenomenon was due to "self-deception resulting from unconscious motor movements guided by expectation."

In the early scientific period, the spiritualist Dawson E. Rogers determined to give a new kind of respectability to spiritualism and to that end founded the Society for Psychical Research (SPR) in 1882. Branches of the SPR were shortly to follow in several European countries, and throughout the United States. When the SPR was founded in 1882, its mission was to find scientific, empirical evidence to disprove the claim of materialism, according to which all phenomena must ultimately submit to the laws governing matter. The SPR pledged to use scientific methods to substantiate its claims, and those were increasingly but not exclusively the methods used by the successful natural sciences. Initially, and during the first phase up to the 1930s, the activities of the SPR covered large surveys, intensive cases and field studies of medium and séances, qualitative studies of precognitive dreams and the like.

The first parapsychology laboratory was that of J. B. Rhine at Duke University in the 1930s.[19]

What we may term the Rhine revolution was a notable feature of the mid-scientific period. In J.B. Rhine's experimental parapsychology laboratory at Duke University, researchers used statistical tools and were able to demonstrate that psychic phenomena are dormant in ordinary people, and not necessarily confined to people who overtly demonstrate such gifts. The term 'parapsychology' came into general use.

J.B.Rhine and Zener began to use what are now known as Zener or ESP cards, which give the guesser a 1 in 5 chance of guessing a card correctly. They settled on a deck of 25 cards. Rhine believed that when someone was found who could do significantly better than 20% in guessing, that would be evidence for telepathy or clairvoyance. Rather than admit that when controls are tightened, it becomes more difficult to deceive investigators, Rhine and other Psi researchers have often concluded that the controls have interfered with the paranormal realm. Some even claim that tight controls make the exercise of psychic power so difficult that it extinguishes it altogether in cases of severe scrutiny, such as when a trained expert in detecting deception is brought in. Experimenter control destroys trust and trust seems necessary for psychic powers to work, according to many Psi researchers.

By the second half of the twentieth century, protocols in Psi research had become much more sophisticated than in its early years. Advances in technology would significantly reduce some of the earlier problems with data recording, randomization, sensory leakage, and so on. In the 1960s, physicist Helmut Schmidt started using random event generators to do micro-PK experiments.

From 1966 to 1972, there were several dream telepathy experiments at Maimonides Medical Centre in Brooklyn, New York, conducted by Montague Ullman and Stanley Krippner. From 1972to 1994, there were a few remote viewing experiments, primarily at the Stanford Research Institute (SRI), which was "a scientific think tank affiliated with Stanford University." Many authors say that it was funded by the CIA. Remote viewing program finally closed in 1994. The CIA shut it down because they were convinced that after 24 years of experiments it was clear that remote viewing was of no practical value to the intelligence community. The CIA report noted that in the case of remote viewing there was a large amount of irrelevant, erroneous information that was provided and there was little agreement observed among the reports of the remote viewers.[20]

Today, decades of well-controlled and methodologically correct laboratory experiments by over 200 researchers in some 27 nations have convinced many about the factual existence of Psi, though the laws according to which such a phenomenon occur are not understood. There have been several experiments in extra sensory perception, namely in telepathy, clairvoyance and precognition, which would indicate that these faculties are normal but unused human potentials and that their use might under some circumstances be deliberately trigged or induced by various means for special purposes. Experiments have been conducted in the United States, Russia, and Eastern Europe by recognized scientists, using standard controlled experimental methods and quantitative statistical computations of results. They should be repeatable experiments provided that all necessary parametric factors are considered. The results have been calculated as successful or highly significant in the cases reported.

The first well attested laboratory experiment on telekinesis was done by J.B. Rhine of Duke University. They actively tried to will two dice to fall so that the total of their sides added up to more than seven. There are 36 possible combinations of two dice, and fifteen of these are greater than seven so that they expected to hit their target 2810 times out of 6744 throws. They scored 3110 which was so far from chance coincidence that it could occur only once in well over a billion times. Rhine's tests, when assessed by his own statistical methods, show an overall significance at a high level of chance. The success of every person being tested shows fluctuations during an experiment. Taken together, these experiments suggest that for dice at least there is evidence of a force of mental origin that can influence the movement of physical objects.

## The Claims of Para-Psychologists

I shall summarize the major claims of the Psi researchers. After each statement I shall give the name of one of the researchers in the field.

1.  Human ESP faculties, telepathy, clairvoyance, precognition etc. can be used to receive or communicate information accurately in various altered states of consciousness (J.B. Rhine).

2.  A psychic phenomenon seems to be more prevalent in primitive peoples and tribals whose world-views accommodate them (Robert Van De Castle).

3.  Problem solving can be enhanced by control over brain–wave function gained by meditative or auto-hypotonic conditionings without the use of EEG or other machines. This involves the use of mental imagery (The Silva Method).

4.  The conditions favourable to ESP may be self-induced and /or induced in others through auto-hypnosis, yoga, meditation, bio-feedback, and various other psychic development programme (Montague Ullman).

5.  Hypnotic-type suggestions, under some circumstances, can be projected and transmitted to others by telepathic means and influence their behaviour.

6.  It is possible to learn to control the alteration of one's own states of consciousness by various methods and techniques and to attain various degrees of conscious control over the automatic body system, eliminate pain sensations, control

bleeding, alter metabolic functions, and accelerate natural healing process of the body (Elmer Green).

7. Psychic healing is possible, and one may be trained to do it by proper mind techniques (Lawrence Le Shan).

8. Certain people have been able to affect the rate of growth in plant and rate of wound healing in mice under rigidly controlled laboratory conditions (Bernard Grad).

9. Certain people can move objects and /or change the properties of matter like Uri Geller, Mathew Manning, and Nelya Sergeyevna (Harold Puthoff).

10. Through some unknown energy fields, physical objects and places can be impregnated with record of thoughts, images, emotions and intentions of persons and events and can be later read or reconstituted as in the art of psychometric or object reading by psychics (Colin Wilson).

## Various kinds of Evidence available for Parapsychology

Although Psi refers to real events, a great deal of superstition, misperception, distorted belief and just plain nonsense under the label of misperception and distorted belief exist in Psi. Scientific method is basically a technique or disciplined style of observing and thinking in order to refine knowledge. We start with the assumption that we know something about those territories of the world we are interested in. Our knowledge is a set of mental maps, concepts and theories about the nature of the reality that direct our dealings with reality. To deal with it most effectively, we need extremely accurate maps of the region we are going to function in. But our present maps are sketchy and contain many errors and blank spots. We need to refine them. And the first step to refine it depends on the kind of evidence available.

There are three basic types of evidence involved in Parapsychological research:

1.  Anecdotal Evidence: The stories of ordinary witnesses about paranormal events which are usually uncritical and has the tendency to become embroidered with the passing time. However, without the anecdotal tradition, there would be no critical study of the paranormal. Furthermore, the anecdotal tradition through the convergence of witnesses can at times be a solid base for study.

2.  Controlled experimental base for study: This is the type of evidence which has been studied under controlled laboratory conditions. Also, systematic efforts have been made to reduplicate the experiment.

3.  Spontaneous Experimental evidence: This consists of data which cannot be strictly controlled, for example, an apparition or a poltergeist display. However, it is called 'experimental,' because at least one trained observer or investigator is present.

## Conditions Favouring PSI Phenomena

Psi researchers claim that the following conditions help in producing Psi phenomena:

1.  Physical relaxation.

2.  Reduced physical arousal or activation.

3.  Reduction is sensory input and processing.

4.  Increased awareness of internal process, feelings, and images.

5.  Receptive mode/right hemisphere functioning as opposed to action mode/left hemispheric functioning.

6.  An altered view of the nature of the world, especially one in which the unity and interrelatedness of the cosmos is emphasized; the concept of time in changed and the usual sense of time is no longer real to one: it is felt to be possible to know things more directly than we usually consider possible; and many of our usual evaluations of events in the world are changed.

Morris, R. Identified 10 areas of potential difficulties facing parapsychology as it approached the last decade of the 20th century:[21]

1.  Parapsychology is linked to problematic metaphysical origins.

2.  Parapsychology is lined with concepts that have been exploited and misused in the past.

3.  Parapsychology can be easily linked with delusional systems.

4.  Parapsychology threatens the tidiness of our scientific methodology.

5.  Parapsychology forces us to look at some theoretical concepts that science has found problematic in the past.

6.  Parapsychology threatens fixed beliefs about how the world works.

7.  Parapsychology's most obvious potential research projects often raise ethical issues.

8.  Parapsychology involves the study of complex, open systems.

9.  Parapsychology has difficulty in generating and testing theory-based hypotheses.

10. Parapsychology has often been labelled a pseudo-science by philosophers and sociologists of science.

The conclusions of many of the experiments in Parapsychology have been well summarized as follows[22]:

1. They produced too many deviations from statistical expectation to be seen only as chance variations.

2. But those deviations were often not reproducible at will under controlled experimental conditions in *replications or by others.*

It is this double pattern of seemingly contradictory results that has both inspired and harassed parapsychology in nearly all cases, where strict experimental research has been employed.

## Conclusion

The original agenda of Parapsychology has been taken over by transpersonal psychology and spirituality. It seems that the paranormal is often experienced in settings with a strong spiritual engagement or by people who conceptualize life in a different way. *Spirituality* re-emerges as the new topic and it is important to acknowledge that it was also at the base of the SPR founding fathers' intentions in 1882.

We need to concede, that the paranormal faculties of the human mind open to human beings a range of experiences which seem to be supernatural. It is the cumulative supernatural experience of the ages, perceived by means of the paranormal faculties sporadically developed in mankind that forms the subject-matter of occult science and the data for its speculations. It is the sporadic development of the paranormal faculties, however, that makes evidential proof a difficulty. Natural science lays its evidence before the five physical senses possessed by every normal human being. Occult science makes its appeal to the judgment of senses but rarely to be found developed in human beings. Ordinary people must base their opinion in occult matters upon circumstantial evidence. Occult science reserves itself for the few whose training and natural gifts enable them to appreciate it. Many people have had experiences which have set them thinking and asking questions. They have glimpsed something outside the four walls of our everyday life, and they are no longer contented with the statement that nothing exists save that which we habitually see.

It must, however, always be kept in mind that occult is a vast range of experience, and it is this body of experience that seeks to systematise and explain. We can look at occult as an extension of psychology, for it studies certain little-known aspects of the human mind. Its findings, rightly formulated and understood, fit in with what is already established in psychology and natural sciences. This mutual corroboration must be the test of occult science. There must be no discrepancies between its findings and those of natural sciences upon such points as natural science is able to test. We must no longer content ourselves with wild statements of psychic experiences in proof of which no shadow of independent evidence can be offered. From time immemorial the training and teaching of specially selected individuals have gone on with making use of altered states of consciousness to go beyond normal functioning of human beings and the schools dedicated to that work are known as the Mystery Schools. Experience of the rarer forms of natural phenomena brings the conviction that their influences, in a subtle and little-understood fashion, affect normal human life very much more than is realised, especially in the spheres of disease and therapeutics.

# Endnotes

[1] Edwards, Frank. "The Man With The X-Ray Mind." *Stranger than Science.* New York, L.Stuart,1959, p.213-16

[2] http://www.directionjournal.org/29/2/occult-roars-back-its-modern-resurgence.html#Note2

[3] Times; The Occult: a substitute faith, June 19, 1972

[4] http://www.directionjournal.org/29/2/occult-roars-back-its-modern-resurgence.html#Note3

[5] The Potter phenomenon." news.bbc.co.uk. BBC. 18 Feb. 2003

[6] J.K. Rowling by the numbers, usatoday.com. USA TODAY. 25 Sept. 2012

[7] J. K. Rowling, Harry Potter and the Philosopher's Stone, Bloomsbury, UK, 1987, p.17

[8] J. K. Rowling, Harry Potter and the Philosopher's Stone, Bloomsbury, UK, 1987, p.45

[9] Rev 13:18

[10] Quoted in Mircea Eliade, *Occultism, Witchcraft and Cultural Fashions* (Chicago, IL: University of Chicago Press, 1976), 48

[11] Robert Galbreath, "The History of Modern Occultism: A Bibliographical Survey," *Journal of Popular Culture* 5 (Winter 1971): 726-5

[12] Marcello Truzzi, "Definition and Dimensions of the Occult: Towards a Sociological Perspective," in *On the Margin of the Visible*, ed. Edward A. Tiryakian (New York: John Wiley, 1974), 244-245

[13] Andrew M. Greeley, "Implications for the Sociology of Religion of Occult Behavior in the Youth Culture," in *On the Margin of the Visible*, 297-98

[14] Ronald Enroth, "The Occult," in *Evangelical Dictionary of Theology*, ed. Walter A. Elwell Grand Rapids, MI: Baker, 1984, 787

[15] Martin E. Marty, "The Occult Establishment," *A Nation of Behavers*, University of Chicago Press, 1976, 135, 139-40

[16] Eliade Mircea, *Occultism, Witchcraft and cultural fashions*, University of Chicago Press, p.67

[17] Weber Max, *The Sociology of Religion* , Beacon Press, Boston,1963, p.270

[18] www.parapsych.org

[19] Pleasants, H. (ed.). *Biographical Dictionary of Parapsychology*, Garrett/ Helix, New York, 1964

[20] Marks, David. *The Psychology of the Psychic*. Prometheus Books, New York, 2000, p.77

[21] 1990-1991, Parapsychology in the 1990's: Addressing the challenge, *European journal of parapsychology*, 8,1-26

[22] Harald Walach, Niko Kohls, Nikolaus von Stillfried, Thilo Hinterberger, Stefan Schmidt, Spirituality: The Legacy of Parapsychology, Archive for the Psychology of Religion 31, 2009 277-308

# Chapter 2

# Altered States of Consciousness (ASC)

Consciousness has baffled neuroscientists for many years. The problem of consciousness is how a kilogram or so of nerve cells conjures up the seamless kaleidoscope of sensations, thoughts, memories and emotions that occupy every waking moment. Most experts think that consciousness can be divided into two parts: the experience of consciousness (or personal awareness), and the contents of consciousness, which include things such as thoughts, beliefs, sensations, perceptions, intentions, memories and emotions.

The human brain is the main organ of the human central nervous system. Mind is a set of cognitive faculties that enable consciousness, perception, thinking, judgment and memory of human beings. Such faculties are also present in other life forms at different levels in comparison to human mind.[1]

Despite all the improvements in our ability to understand the human brain, we still have no explanation for how the brain creates consciousness. The standard materialist position is that consciousness is tied up with the brain. There is plenty of evidence that the brain influences consciousness, ranging from studies of brain damage to the well-known effects of mind-altering chemicals. The problem with going any further than this correlational fact is that no one knows how to define consciousness from an objective, third-person perspective. We only have access to *one* consciousness: our own. Every other consciousness is in a sense inferred from behaviour. We treat people as conscious because they *seem* conscious to us, and this *seeming* is a product of both our evolved perceptual systems and the cultural systems that operate on top of them.

## Altered States of Consciousness (ASC)

An **altered state of consciousness** is a temporary change in one's normal mental state without being considered unconscious. Altered states of consciousness can be created intentionally, or they can happen by accident or due to illness.

Everyone has experienced dreams and can relate to this common altered state of consciousness. Although we are not 'awake' during sleep, we are still conscious and can react to our surroundings. During sleep, we experience images, sounds, and feelings that are not real. Many dreams are forgotten after waking, but we all know that dreams can feel very real when we are in them. Daydreaming is also considered an altered state of consciousness. Other ASC are: hypnosis, meditation, hallucination and trance states. They can also come about accidentally through indigestion, fever, sleep deprivation, starvation, oxygen deprivation, or a traumatic accident.

The key to understanding occult experience is to explore altered states of consciousness. To briefly paraphrase the last several thousand years of development in the magical arts, "magic" is achieved by first attaining an altered state in which the subconscious and reality itself is susceptible to reprogramming, and then firing a desire in symbolized form into the subconscious. Occult phenomena have a long tradition of being associated with alterations of consciousness. This tradition extends from the performances of ancient oracles and other diviners to the mesmeric and mediumistic trance, and to more recent claims in the context of laboratory work that used hypnotic suggestion, dreams, meditation, and partial sensory deprivation. Moreover, there has been a long tradition of spontaneous ESP experiences related to dreams and other states of consciousness that have reinforced such associations.

Today there is a proliferation of techniques that **induce altered states of consciousness** — most stem from traditional sources, some combined with techniques from modern research. Meditation, yoga, tantra, drumming, chanting, ecstatic dance, hypnosis, sensory deprivation, and chemical substances among many others are widely available and much publicized. Often these practices are accompanied by psychophysical and "mystical" phenomena.

In the New Age Religions, devotees believe that they need only to get their consciousness attuned to the same frequency as that of the Universal Consciousness. Thus, salvation comes by doing all manner of things to alter the normal state of consciousness, such as Meditation, Drug use, Hypnosis, chanting, doing ecstatic dance movements, and so forth. So, making a human person whole becomes merely a matter of Spiritual Technology or of doing Scientific Procedures, causing one to achieve an altered state of consciousness, enabling the participant to consciously or 'mystically' experience a union with the Universal Consciousness.

Some of the techniques are mainly used to work on the body, such as ecstatic dance movements and the use of body flotation therapy, while others are designed to work on the mind, such as Meditation and hypnosis. The New Age Adherents truly believe that these Altered States of Consciousness are a positive means of opening oneself to beneficial psychological and spiritual influences. They really do believe that by inducing these trance-like states that their spirituality is being aided by helping them to progress into their full potential to become 'gods!'

The methods for inducing a trance state or altered conscious state vary, but generally include listening to specific audio tones or viewing visual stimuli designed to entrain the brain for the purpose of altering the person's mood or perceptions. Other methods include total sensory deprivation, where the subject isolates himself as much as possible from all external stimuli, usually with the intent of inducing hallucinations. The human mind abhors a vacuum and will generate false stimuli or hallucinations if necessary to avoid having none. Of course, some use specific drugs to aid in the mood-altering process.

Some people have experimented with trances and altered states of consciousness as a means to broaden their awareness, others say it helps them feel "one with God". Lasting changes in personality, a lingering sense of detachment and other undesirable changes can result if trance states or other sensory modifications are undertaken too often, especially if drugs are involved. Then, there is the addictive nature that comes with anything that feels good, keeping a person away from spending their time with friends and family and so on.

## Mind States

By connecting a subject to an Electroencephalograph (EEG), his/her brain waves can be measured in cycles per second (c.p.s.). This is not so much a quantitative measure of mental activity as it is of a state of mind. There are essentially four states - beta, alpha, theta and delta.

At an average of 20 c.p.s., the beta state is the normal, everyday waking state. In this state we are predominantly engaged in left brain activity. Lowering the brain wave frequency to around 12 c.p.s. brings us into the alpha state, and it is here that right brain activity is engaged. Lowering frequency simply means cutting out unnecessary stress and brain 'chit-chat'. Besides engaging creative abilities, this makes the individual more alert, allows clearer thinking and enables mental faculties which the beta level does not.

Beta (13–30 cycles per second): This brain wave indicates that our conscious mind is in control. It indicates a mental state of logical thought, analysis, and action. We are alert and awake talking, speaking, doing, solving problems, and so on. Beta brain waves are associated with normal waking consciousness and a heightened state of alertness, logic and critical reasoning. Higher Beta levels translate into stress, anxiety and restlessness.

Alpha (7–12 cycles per second): This brain wave indicates relaxation and meditation. It is a state of relaxed alertness: good for inspiration, and learning facts fast. Alpha brain waves are present in deep relaxation with the eyes usually closed and while day-dreaming. The relaxed detached awareness achieved during light meditation is characteristic of Alpha and is optimal for programming our mind for success. Alpha heightens our imagination, visualization, memory, learning and concentration.

Theta (4–8 cycles per second): This is a state of deep meditation. This is best for suggestibility and inspiration. This brain wave is dominant in children of age 2–5. Theta brain waves are present during deep meditation and light sleep, including the Rapid Eye Movement dream state. Theta is the realm of our subconscious mind. A sense of deep spiritual connection and oneness with the Universe can be experienced at Theta.

Delta (0.5–4 cycles per second): This is a state of deep dreamless sleep and deep relaxation. The Delta frequency is the slowest and is present in deep, dreamless sleep. Delta is associated with deep healing and regeneration, underlining the importance of deep sleep to the healing process.

Many people attain the state of relaxed attention with daily meditation or relaxing exercises, especially deep breathing. But more and more people are convinced that some types of music or chanting can achieve the results much quicker and easier. Certain types of musical rhythms help relax the body, calm the breath, and evoke a gentle state of relaxed awareness which is highly receptive to learning new information.

Researchers who study aspects of human consciousness have suggested that within the course of a single day an individual may flicker in and out of several states of consciousness. Some theorize that there are six states of "nonreflective consciousness," characterized by the absence of self-consciousness. These states include:

1. Bodily feelings, which are induced by normal bodily functioning and are characterized by nonreflective awareness in the organs and tissues of the digestive, glandular, respiratory, and other bodily systems. This awareness does not become self-conscious unless such stimuli as pain or hunger intensify a bodily feeling.

2. Stored memories, which do not become self-conscious until the individual reactivates them.

3. Coma, which is induced by illness, epileptic seizures, or physical injuries to the brain, and is characterized by prolonged nonreflective consciousness of the entire organism.

4.  Stupor, which is induced by psychosis, narcotics, or over-indulgence in alcohol, and is characterized by greatly reduced ability to perceive incoming sensations.

5.  Non-rapid-eye-movement sleep, which is caused by a normal part of the sleep cycle at night or during daytime naps and is characterized by a minimal amount of mental activity, which may sometimes be recalled upon awakening.

6.  Rapid-eye-movement sleep, which is a normal part of the night-time sleep cycle and is characterized by the mental activity known as dreams.

The following can be considered as altered states of consciousness:

1.  Rapturous consciousness, characterized by intense feelings and overpowering emotions induced by sexual stimulation, the fervour of religious conversion, or the ingestion of certain drugs.

2.  Hysterical consciousness, induced by rage, jealousy, fear, neurotic anxiety, violent mob activity, or certain drugs. As opposed to rapturous consciousness, which is generally evaluated as pleasant and positive in nature, hysterical consciousness is considered negative and destructive.

3.  Fragmented consciousness, defined as a lack of integration among important segments of the total personality, often resulting in psychosis, severe neurosis, amnesia, multiple personality, or dissociation. Such a state of consciousness is induced by severe psychological stress over a period. It may also be brought about temporarily by accidents or psychedelic drugs.

4.  Relaxed consciousness, characterized by a state of minimal mental activity, passivity, and an absence of motor activity. This state of consciousness may be brought about by lack of external stimulation, such as sunbathing, floating in water or being under the influence of certain drugs.

5.  Daydreaming, induced by boredom, social isolation, or sensory deprivation.

6.  Trance consciousness, induced by rapt attentiveness to a single stimulus, such as the voice of a hypnotist, one's own heartbeat, a chant, certain drugs, or trance-inducing rituals and primitive dances. The trance state is characterized by hyper suggestibility and concentrated attention on one stimulus to the exclusion of all others.

7.  Expanded consciousness, comprising four levels: a) the sensory level, characterized by subjective reports of space, time, body image, or sense impressions having been altered; b) the recollective-analytic level, which summons up memories of one's past and provides insights concerning self, work, or personal relationships; c) the symbolic level, which is often characterized by vivid visual imagery of mythical, religious, and historical symbols; d) the integrative level, in which the individual undergoes an intense religious illumination, experiences a dissolution of self, and is confronted by God or some divine being. Each of these four levels might be induced by psychedelic drugs, hypnosis, meditation, prayer, or free association during psychoanalysis. Through the ages, many of humankind's major material and spiritual breakthroughs may have come from these virtually unmapped, uncharted regions of the mind.

The term "altered state of consciousness" was introduced and defined by Arnold Ludwig in 1966. An altered state of consciousness is any mental state induced by physiological, psychological or pharmacological manoeuvres or agents, which deviate from the normal waking state of consciousness. Some observable abnormal and sluggish behaviour meet the criteria for altered state of consciousness. It is a temporary change in one's normal mental state without being considered unconscious. Ludwig has done a classification of altered states of consciousness as given below[2]:

## A.  *Reduction of External Stimuli*

These include mental states resulting primarily from the absolute reduction of sensory input as in

- solitary confinement

- extreme boredom states

- sleep and related phenomena, such as dreaming and somnambulism

- experimental sensory deprivation states.

## B.  *Increase of External Stimuli and Emotion*

Under this category are included excitatory mental states resulting primarily from sensory overload or bombardment

- suggestible mental states produced by grilling or "third degree" tactics

- brainwashing states

- hyperkinetic trance associated with emotional contagion encountered in a group or mob setting; religious conversion and healing trance experiences

- spirit possession states

- shamanistic and prophetic trance states during tribal ceremonies

- fire walker's trance

- orgiastic trance, experienced by Satanists during certain religious rites

- ecstatic trance, such as experienced by the "howling" or "whirling" dervishes, depersonalization, panic states, rage reactions, hysterical conversion reactions, bewitchment, and demoniacal possession states

- acute psychotic states such as schizophrenic reactions.

## C.   *Increased Alertness or Mental Involvement*

- prolonged vigilance during sentry duty; prolonged observation of a radar screen

- fervent praying

- intense mental absorption in a task, such as reading, writing, or problem solving

- total mental involvement in listening to a dynamic or charismatic speaker

- the prolonged watching of a revolving drum, metronome, or stroboscope.

## D.   *Decreased Alertness or Relaxation of Critical Faculties*

- mystical, transcendental, or revelatory states attained through passive meditation or occurring spontaneously during the relaxation of one's critical faculties

- mediumistic and auto-hypnotic trances

- profound aesthetic experiences; creative, illuminatory, and insightful states

- free associative states during psychoanalytic therapy

- reading-trance, especially reading poetry

- nostalgia, music-trance resulting from absorption in soothing lullabies or musical scores

- mental states associated with profound cognitive and muscular relaxation, such as during floating on water or sun-bathing.

### E.  *Presence of Somato-Psychological Factors*

- hypoglycemia, either spontaneous or subsequent to fasting;

- hyperglycemia, dehydration, thyroid and adrenal gland dysfunctions

- sleep deprivation

- hyperventilation, narcolepsy, and temporal lobe seizures

In addition, ASCs may be induced through the administration of numerous pharmacological agents, such as anaesthetics and psychedelic, narcotic, sedative, and stimulant drugs.

## General Characteristics of ASCs

Although ASCs share many features in common, there are certain general moulding influences which appear to account for much of their apparent differences in outward manifestation and subjective experience. Despite the apparent differences among ASCs, we shall find that there are several common denominators whose features allow us to conceptualize these ASCs as somewhat related phenomena.

1. Alterations in thinking. Subjective disturbances in concentration, attention, memory, and judgment represent common findings. Archaic modes of thought (primary process thought) predominate, and reality testing seems impaired to varying degrees. The distinction between cause and effect becomes blurred, and ambivalence may be pronounced whereby incongruities or opposites may coexist without any logical conflict.

2. Disturbed time sense. Sense of time and chronology become greatly altered. Subjective feelings of timelessness, time coming to a standstill, the acceleration or slowing of time, and so on, are common. Time may also seem of infinite or infinitesimal duration.

3. Loss of control. People entering an ASC, often experience fears of losing their grip on reality and losing their self-control. During the induction phase, they may actively try to resist experiencing the ASCs (e.g., sleep, hypnosis, anaesthesia), while in other instances they may welcome relinquishing his volition and giving into the experience (e.g., narcotic drugs, alcohol, LSD, mystical states). The experience of "loss of control" is a complicated phenomenon. Relinquishing conscious control may arouse feelings of impotency and helplessness, or paradoxically may represent the gaining of greater control and power through the loss of control. This latter experience may be found in hypnotized persons This is also the case in mystical, revelatory, or in spirit possession states wherein the person relinquishes conscious control in the hope of experiencing divine truths, clairvoyance, "cosmic consciousness," communion with the spirits or supernatural powers, or serving as a temporary abode or mouthpiece for the gods.

4. Change in emotional expression. Sudden and unexpected displays of more primitive and intense emotion than shown during normal, waking consciousness may appear. Emotional extremes commonly occur, ranging from ecstasy and orgiastic equivalents to profound fear and depression. There is another pattern of emotional expression which may characterize these states. The individual may become detached, uninvolved, or relate intense feelings without any emotional display.

5. Body image change. A wide array of distortions in body image frequently occurs in ASCs. There is also a common propensity for individuals to experience a profound sense of depersonalization, a schism between body and mind, feelings of de-realization, or a dissolution of boundaries between self and others, the world, or universe.

6. Perceptual distortions. Common to most ASCs is the presence of perceptual aberrations, including hallucinations, pseudo-hallucinations, increased visual imagery, subjectively felt hyper-acuteness of perception, and illusions of every variety. The content of these perceptual aberrations may be determined by cultural, group, individual, or neurophysiological factors.

In some ASCs, such as those produced by psychedelic drugs, or mystical contemplation, synaesthesia may appear whereby one form of sensory experience is translated into another form. For example, persons may report seeing or feeling sounds or being able to taste what they see. Nitrous oxide when sufficiently diluted with air, stimulate the mystical consciousness in an extraordinary degree. Depth upon depth of truth seems revealed to the inhaler. This truth fades out, however, or escapes now the inhaler comes back to normal consciousness.

7. Sense of the ineffable. Most often, because of the uniqueness of the subjective experience associated with certain ASCs (e.g., transcendental, aesthetic, creative, psychotic, and mystical states), persons claim a certain ineptness or inability to communicate the nature or the essence of the experience to someone who has not undergone a similar experience. Contributing to the sense of the ineffable is the tendency of persons to develop varying degrees of amnesia for their experiences during profound alterations of consciousness, such as hypnotic trance, somnambulistic trance, possession fits, dreams, mystical experiences, delirious states, drug intoxications, aura, orgiastic and ecstatic states, and the like.

8. Feelings of rejuvenation. Upon emerging from certain profound alterations of consciousness through psychedelic experiences, abreactive states due to the administration of carbon dioxide, methamphetamine, ether, hypnosis, religious conversion, transcendental and mystical states, insulin coma therapy, spirit possession fits, primitive puberty rites, and even, on some occasions, deep sleep, many persons claim to experience a new sense of hope, rejuvenation, renaissance, or rebirth.

9. Hyper-suggestibility. Increased susceptibility and propensity of persons to accept uncritically and/or automatically to respond to specific or nonspecific statements. Hyper-suggestibility will also refer to the increased tendency of a person to misperceive or misinterpret various stimuli or situations based either on his inner fears or wishes.

## Functions of ASCs

Now that we have considered certain characteristics associated with ASCs, we might raise the question whether they serve any useful biological, psychological, or social functions of man. The widespread occurrence and use of mystical and possession states or aesthetic and creative experiences indicates that these ASCs satisfy many needs of both man and society.

1.  Healing: Throughout history, the production of ASCs has played a major role in the various healing arts and practices. The induction of these states has been employed for almost every conceivable aspect of psychological therapy. During the actual treatment or healing ceremony, the shaman, medicine man, priest, physician, or psychiatrist may view the production of an ASC in the patient as a crucial prerequisite for healing. There are countless instances of healing practices designed to take advantage of the suggestibility, increased meaning, propensity for emotional catharsis, and the feelings of rejuvenation associated with ASCs. The faith cures at Lourdes and other religious shrines, the healing through prayer and meditation, cures by the "healing touch," the laying on of hands, encounters with religious relics, spiritual healing, spirit possession cures, exorcism, mesmeric or magnetic treatment, and modern-day hypnotherapy are all obvious instances of the role of ASCs in treatment.

2.  Avenues of new knowledge or experience: Human beings often have sought to induce ASCs to gain new knowledge, inspiration, or experience. In the realm of religion, intense prayer, passive meditation, revelatory and prophetic states, mystical and transcendental experiences, religious conversion, and divination states have served human beings

in opening new realms of experience, reaffirming moral
values, resolving emotional conflicts, and often enabling
them to cope better with their human predicaments and
the world about them. It is also interesting to note that
among many primitive groups, spirit possession is believed
to impart a superhuman knowledge which could not possibly
be gained during waking consciousness. Such paranormal
faculties as supernatural wisdom, the "gift of tongues,"
and clairvoyance are supposedly demonstrated during the
possession fit.

I like to quote a very pertinent remark of William James.[3] "Our
normal waking consciousness . . . is but one special type of
consciousness, whilst all about it, parted from it by the filmiest
of screens, there lie potential forms of conscious entirely
different. We may go through life without suspecting their
existence; but apply the requisite stimulus, and at a touch they
are all there in all their completeness, definite types of mentality
which probably somewhere have their field of application and
adaptation. No account of the universe in its totality can be
final which leaves these other forms of consciousness quite
disregarded. How to regard them is the question for they are
so discontinuous with ordinary consciousness. Yet, they may
determine attitudes though they cannot furnish formulas, and
open a region though they fail to give a map. At any rate, they
forbid a premature closing of our accounts with reality."

## The Dangers of Altered States of Consciousness
There are clearly risks to cultivating altered states:

> First, ASCs may induce mental illness in unstable individuals, or
> they may naturally progress into mental illness. Because no one can
> predict if this will occur, the risk is like that of taking powerful,
> experimental drugs. Arnold M. Ludwig, writing in Charles Tart's

*Altered States of Consciousness*, observes, "As a person enters or is in an ASC, he often experiences fear of losing his grip on reality and losing his self-control[4]. More and more psychologists who personally explore states of consciousness are now blurring the distinction between sanity and insanity and reinterpreting psychopathological conditions as a form of "higher consciousness."

Second, altered states can open a person to the supernatural realm and contact with spirits whose effect on consciousness cannot be predicted. No one can logically deny that a legitimate connection exists between altered states of consciousness and spirit influence or spirit possession. There are many cases of such instances of attempted or successful possession to be found in the literature on spiritualism, magic, witchcraft and madness. Such visitations are by no means restricted to those who have ingested a psychedelic agent—they are potentially available to anyone who has entered this region of consciousness by whatever means. Many of the claims made by mental patients that they are possessed by alien entities are best understood as representing a perfectly accurate assessment of what has happened to them in an altered state of consciousness.

A third problem with altered states is their ability to profoundly affect one's perception. For example, the goal of most ASC programs is the destruction of the limited personal self to uncover the alleged expanded Self. People attempting to expand the gates of perception by taking psychedelics and other means may end up destroying their normal functional state of consciousness. Leading consciousness researcher John White explains: "But the critical point to be understood is this: the value of mystical and transformative states is not in producing some new experience but in *getting rid of the experiencer*. Getting rid, that is, of the egocentric consciousness which experiences life from a contracted, self-centered point of view rather than the free, unbound perspective of a sage who knows he or she is infinity operating through a finite form".[5]

Many of the unusual visual events in altered states are undoubtedly illusions or hallucinations caused by disruptions in the normal cognitive and perceptual operations of the brain. Others may be due to an abnormal activation of brain mechanisms that are responsible for dreaming. Sensory deprivation and Eastern meditation techniques can also affect the operation of neurons to a certain extent, because both states can apparently alter the electrical patterns (EEGs) that emanate from the brain. There are several phenomena that might be created through interference with the neuronal operations that underlie perception.

Altered states also have important commonalities. They can all impair one's ability to test reality, to think critically and logically or to remember. They create a passive state in which mental events seem to develop on their own and are simply experienced rather than being controlled. Many also weaken emotional restraints, allowing moods to swing from wild jubilation to deep fear and depression. In addition, they can all create perceptual distortions and hallucinations and precipitate unusual bodily sensations like numbness, dizziness, tingling or rushes of energy. They can make people hyper suggestible, so they are open to many strange beliefs and are easily influenced by the suggestions of other people. Altered states have the singular ability to make all kinds of improbable events seem exceptionally real and significant. One final effect of altered states is their apparent ability to facilitate or enhance mystical experience.

## Trance

A remarkable characteristic feature of the hypnotic trance is that hypnotized persons become highly suggestible or easily influenced by the suggestions or instructions of others, generally the hypnotist. They retain their powers to act and can walk, talk, speak, and respond to questions. Their perceptions, however, can be radically altered or distorted.

A stage hypnotist tells his mesmerized subject, a dignified woman in a designer dress: "When I snap my fingers, you will run in circles and bark like a dog." Moments later, the woman is out of the trance and chatting happily about the experience, when suddenly the hypnotist snaps his fingers. The woman instantly begins running in circles and barking, and the audience breaks into howls of laughter.

A psychiatrist turns down the room light. He takes a beautiful pen with an unusual golden cap from his pocket and begins wagging it back and forth in front of his client's eyes. He intones: "As you watch the pen, you are feeling sleepy. Your eyes are becoming heavy . . . ." Moments later, in a deep trance, the client begins exploring traumatic moments of her childhood, guided by the skilled psychiatrist.

This is our image of trance: a special state of mind, induced by a skilled professional, over which the subject has little control.

Yet the father of modern hypnotherapy, Milton Erickson, insisted that trance was a quite common state, one that we drop into many times a day without any help at all - a "petting the kitty" trance, a "yelling at the kids" trance, a "lovemaking" trance, a "getting dressed down by my superiors" trance, etc..

How can we call these events "trances" when they are so ordinary? Erickson pointed out several key ingredients of a trance -- and it is these defining ingredients that give the trance state its great power. These might be pleasant or unpleasant experiences, they might be helpful to us or they may be holding us back, but they have several things in common:

- Trance is an altered state of consciousness in which the attention is narrowed, focused for the moment just on the purring kitty, on the face and body of the loved one, on the outraged boss. Other inputs -- the birds chirping outside, the itch they had a moment ago, their worry about the big meeting at lunch -- tend to fade in importance. In fact, these may not be registered at all.

- A trance feels autonomous, like something that is happening to them. It does not feel like they are creating it -- yet they are. As a corollary, their behaviour while in the trance feels automatic, autonomous, out of their control. They don't start it, they can't stop it, and they can't change it -- at least, that's how it feels, and that's how they act.

- A trance comes packaged with any of several "Deep Trance Phenomena." Shifted time is one such phenomenon, in which we can regress to a childlike state (the enraged superior becomes mapped onto a domineering father), or project ourselves into an imagined future ("I'm going to lose my job!").

- A trance tends to repeat. A trance is a package of learned skills and trance phenomena triggered by some outside stimulus.

## Placebo Effect and Healing

A *placebo* is a treatment that is expected to have no inherent pharmacological or physical benefit—for instance, a sugar capsule given for anxiety or pain, or a distilled water injection for fever or a sham surgery in which the critical surgical procedure is not performed. Placebos are typically inactive substances which are physically indistinguishable from active medications, though active placebos are occasionally used. Placebos were originally considered to be futile substances, as is evident in early definitions of the placebo as "medicines prescribed more to please the patient than for therapeutic effectiveness."[6] Malani[7] describes placebos as medications for which patient responses depend on their expectations regarding the value of the treatment, while Giordano[8] defines a placebo as "any intervention, event, or experience that evokes positive subjective or objective outcomes in a patient."

Placebos are often used for comparison in clinical studies, as a baseline against which we evaluate the efficacy of investigational clinical treatments. However, placebo treatments often elicit observable improvements on their own in signs or symptoms —these are *placebo effects*. For this reason, placebos have been used as healing agents for a variety of ailments; they have had a place in the healer's repertoire for thousands of years, and they are still used as a viable treatment option by physicians in industrialized countries with surprising frequency. The existence of placebo-induced physiological effects is certainly well established. Placebo effects have been found in the brain, respiratory system, cardiovascular system and immune system.[9] Several studies of various psychotherapeutic interventions have found that their effectiveness can be largely attributed to placebo responses.[10]

The potential significance of the placebo response has led to the standard use of placebo groups in clinical trials examining the efficacy of medicine or other specific treatments on clinical conditions. Patients are assigned to receive either active treatment or placebo, and comparisons between groups are performed to test whether the active treatment elicits greater improvement than placebo. Two critical assumptions underlie the rationale behind the placebo-controlled clinical trial. First, it is assumed that psychological and nonspecific effects, such as natural course of disease, effects of being in a healing environment, and patient expectation and motivation to heal, have equal effects on outcomes in active treatment and placebo groups. Second, it is assumed that nonspecific effects and treatment effects combine additively, so that subtracting outcomes for the placebo group from the treatment group will reveal the specific effects of the drug or procedure. Although these assumptions may not always hold, the placebo-controlled randomized clinical trial is perhaps the best tool for medical practitioners and pharmaceutical companies to determine treatment efficacy.

Psychologists and neuroscientists are interested, however, in whether and how the psychological components of treatment—expectancies, appraisals, learning, context effects, and the relationship between patient and practitioner—can directly affect the bodily state: what are the effects of the treatment context, and how do they affect physiology? This question can be answered by studying the placebo response. In the clinical context, this can be achieved through a three-arm version of the clinical trial, in addition to the active treatment and placebo groups, a subset of patients is assigned to a "natural history" comparison group that receives no treatment. Comparisons between this no-treatment group and the placebo group allow researchers to avoid many potential statistical artefacts, some of which are described later in this chapter, to assess the placebo response—the active effects of psychological state.

Placebos can produce highly specific effects and there are several theories regarding how they exert their influence. Such theories encompass patient expectation, hope, motivation, therapeutic relationships, conditioned responses and other psychological processes.[11] However, the two most influential components are undoubtedly expectancy and classical conditioning. The role of expectancy, whereby the placebo effect is generated from the anticipation that a treatment will result in a specific outcome, has been verified by a systematic review of 85 studies.[12]

Another principal theory regarding placebo effects concerns motivation. Placebo effects may occur in response to goals, such as the aim to improve health and feel better, or to cooperate with a health care practitioner or an experimenter. In some cases, the expectation or hope of getting better causes individuals to attribute spontaneous recovery, remission or a lessening of symptoms to placebo treatments, or even feel better despite a lack of objective evidence that a condition has been cured or lessened, a misattribution that is most likely to occur with conditions that tend to wax and wane. Improvements in medical or psychological conditions may result from factors other than the administration of active medication or a placebo, such as regression to the mean. People are more inclined to seek treatment when their ailment is at its worst, yet pain tends to be variable and eventually resolves on its own. If an individual has recently sought medical or alternative treatment, he or she is likely to attribute the remission to the treatment provided as opposed to the body's natural healing mechanisms.

With the dawn of the 21st century came a perceptible paradigm shift. Given that placebos can produce beneficial physiological effects and that for some conditions these effects are equivalent to those of the active treatment, many consider whether it is ethical to label inactive substances that produce significant effects as sham treatments and deny them to patients who could plausibly gain real benefits from them.

Psychologists and neuroscientists today are most interested in the *placebo response,* the brain and body response to the psychosocial (and perhaps neurobiological) context surrounding treatment. The study of the placebo response reveals active processes that provide a powerful window into brain - body interactions and the brain substrates of human behaviour.

## Multiple Personality Disorder and ASCs

Multiple Personality Disorder which is also called Dissociative Identity Disorder (DID) is a condition wherein a person's identity is fragmented into two or more distinct personality states.[13] These distinct identities may alternately take control of an individual. This may be very similar to an experience of possession. DID is a severe form of dissociation, a mental process which produces a lack of connection in a person's thoughts, memories, feelings, actions, or sense of identity. If you say that someone has a split personality, you mean that their moods can change so much that they seem to have two separate personalities. Its defining feature is the presence of at least two alternate personalities (alters) who routinely take control of the person's behaviour. A person with DID also experiences noticeable, recurring gaps in their memory.

Multiple Personality Disorder is among the most historic of disorders dating back to ancient forms of shamanism and demonic possession.[14] The idea of multiple identities is present in many cultures but there are distinct differences. For example, shamanism and demonic possession are respected and practiced events in some cultures. There are also similarities between cultures. The major similarity is that these individuals are more influenced by hypnosis and more able to enter a dream state because of their ability to dissociate. Even with some similarities, it suggests that MPD is not cross-cultural. This also raises one of the major criticisms of MPD.

In people with multiple personalities, there is a strong psychological separation between each sub-personality; each will have his own name and age, and often some specific memories and abilities. Frequently, for example, personalities will differ in handwriting, artistic talent or even in knowledge of foreign languages. It is interesting to note that patients have been known to develop more and more alters as the disease goes on. Sometimes patients will start with just 2 or 3 alter personalities and it will develop into nearly one hundred. It is common for those with MPD to have personalities of both sexes.

Multiple personalities typically develop in people who were severely and repeatedly abused as children, apparently to protect themselves against the pain of the abuse. Often only one or two of the sub-personalities will be conscious of the abuse, while others will have no memory or experience of the pain. It is unclear why some abused children develop the syndrome while others do not.

One of the problems for psychiatrists trying to treat patients with multiple personalities is that, depending which personality is in control, a patient can have drastically different reactions to a given psychiatric medication. For instance, it is almost always the case that one or several of the personalities of a given patient will be that of a child. And the differences in responses to drugs among the sub-personalities often parallel those ordinarily found when the same drug at the same dose is given to a child, rather than an adult.

DID reflects a failure to integrate various aspects of identity, memory, and consciousness into a single multidimensional self. Usually, a primary identity carries the individual's given name and is passive, dependent, guilty, and depressed. When in control, each personality state, or alter, may be experienced as if it has a distinct history, self-image and identity. The alters' characteristics—including name, reported age and gender, vocabulary, general knowledge, and predominant mood—contrast with those of the primary identity. Certain circumstances or stressors can cause a alter to emerge. The various identities may deny knowledge of one another, be critical of one another or appear to be in open conflict.

Possession-form identities often manifest as behaviors that appear as if a spirit or other supernatural being has taken control of the person. Many possession states around the world are a normal part of a cultural or spiritual practice; these possession states become a disorder when they are unwanted, cause distress or impairment, and are not accepted as part of a cultural or religious practice.

The disease theory of Multiple Personality Disorder is that unhappiness in adulthood stems from trauma in childhood and the trauma is so severe that the individual creates multiple identities to cope with it.[15] The severe trauma is thought to be a result of physical or sexual abuse in childhood. Likewise, most modern patients are women who have been diagnosed with other disorders before being diagnosed with MPD. This is because the intense trauma caused by abuse may create other disorders as well. Because it is associated with other disorders, it was not long before MPD appeared in the Diagnostic and

Statistical Manual of Mental Disorders. It first appeared in the 3rd edition (DSM-III); however the name was changed to Dissociative Identity Disorder in the DSM-IV (Dunn, 1992).

The diagnosis of DID continues to remain controversial among mental health professionals as understanding of the illness develops, but there is no question that the symptoms are real and people do experience them. The following criteria must be met for an individual to be diagnosed with dissociative identity disorder:

- The individual experiences two or more distinct identities or personality states (each with its own enduring pattern of perceiving, relating to, and thinking about the environment and self). Some cultures describe this as an experience of possession.

- The disruption in identity involves a change in sense of self, sense of agency, and changes in behavior, consciousness, memory, perception, cognition, and motor function.

- Frequent gaps are found in memories of personal history, including people, places, and events, for both the distant and recent past. These recurrent gaps are not consistent with ordinary forgetting.

- These symptoms cause clinically significant distress or impairment in social, occupational, or other important areas of functioning.

Identities may emerge in specific circumstances. Transitions from one identity to another are often triggered by psychosocial stress. In the possession-form cases of dissociative identity disorder, alternate identities are visibly obvious to people around the individual. In non-possession-form cases, most individuals do not overtly display their change in identity for long periods of time.

People with DID may describe feeling that they have suddenly become depersonalized observers of their own speech and actions. They might report hearing voices (a child's voice, the voice of a spiritual power), and in some cases, these voices accompany multiple streams of thought that the individual has no control over. The individual might also experience sudden impulses or strong emotions that they don't feel control or a sense of ownership over. People may also report that their bodies suddenly feel different, or that they experience a sudden shift in attitudes or personal preferences before shifting back.

More than 70 percent of people with DID have attempted suicide, and self-injurious behavior is common among this population. Treatment is crucial to improving quality of life and preventing suicide attempts.

Why some people develop DID is not entirely understood, but they frequently report having experienced severe physical and sexual abuse, particularly during childhood. The disorder may first manifest at any age. Individuals with DID may have post-traumatic symptoms (nightmares, flashbacks, and startle responses) or post-traumatic stress disorder. Several studies suggest that DID is more common among close biological relatives of persons who also have the disorder than in the general population.

A well-adjusted individual is one who adapts to surroundings. If adaptation is not possible, the individual makes realistic efforts to change the situation, using personal talents and abilities constructively and successfully. The well-adjusted person is realistic and able to face facts whether they are pleasant or unpleasant, and deals with them instead of merely worrying about them or denying them. Well-adjusted mature persons are independent. They form reasoned opinions and then act on them. They seek a reasonable amount of information and advice before deciding, and once the decision is made, they are willing to face the consequences of it. They do not try to force others to make decisions for them. An ability to love others is typical of the well-adjusted individual. In addition, the mature well-adjusted person is also able to enjoy receiving love and affection and can accept a reasonable dependence on others.

Although individuals with a personality disorder can function in day-to-day life, they are hampered both emotionally and psychologically by the maladaptive nature of their disorder, and their chances of forming good relationships and fulfilling their potentialities are poor. Despite their problems, these patients refuse to acknowledge that anything is wrong and insist that it is the rest of the world that is out of step. Very often their behavior is extremely annoying to those around them. It is evident that the Personality disorder is caused by changes in consciousness. So, altered states of consciousness is related to Multiple Personality Disorder.

## Lunar Effects

Across the centuries many persons around the world have associated weird nocturnal events with the moon and its different phases. The festivals of many religions are still lunar, including some of the greatest Christian celebrations. Easter is determined by the moon, and subsequently are the various Church celebrations whose date depends on this great religious occasion.

The moon's ability to pull on the sea water was thought also to cause a similar pull on the water contained in our bodies. Not only that, but the full Moon "is claimed to be related to a huge list of human misery, including accidents, alcoholism, anxiety, assaults, calls to crisis telephone numbers, casino activity, depression, domestic violence, drug overdoses and, of course, emergency-room visits."[16]

The peculiar effect of the moon on the minds of men and women has been noted from ancient times. The fuller the moon the more turbulent, excitable and impressionable the mind becomes. It is a commonplace observation among those who must deal with people en masse that there occurs a noticeable increase in unusual, eccentric behaviour during the time of the full moon. The moon is popularly held to have a disturbing effect on the minds of idiots and the insane, and all those who are afflicted with nervous disorders. The word 'lunatic' is derived from the Latin word *luna*, 'moon', thus preserving the basis of the age-old theory.

In folklore and mythology, the waxing moon sends powerful impulses of 'growth' energy to the earth, and this affects all things that grow, causing them to increase in size and energy. Similarly, as the moon wanes or decreases in size, growing things decrease in energy.[17] On the basis of this theory, it is thought that the best time for picking flowers and herbs, and for felling trees for fuel and timber, is when the moon is on the decline. Similarly, trees will bear good fruit, if pruned during the moon's increase. Plants are said to "grow best if sown two days before the full moon, so that they gather strength as the moon grows." Peasants in many ancient communities used to sow by the moon, and there are many gardeners and farmers even today who will plant according to the phases of the moon.

## Emotions and Vibrations

Emotions are a stunning expression of our energy, the "vibe" we give off. We register these with intuition. Some people are good to be around with; they improve our mood and vitality. Others are draining our energy; we instinctively want to get away. This "subtle energy" can be felt inches or feet from the body, though it is invisible. Indigenous cultures honour this energy as life force. In Chinese medicine, it is called *chi*, a vitality that is essential to health. Though the molecular structure of subtle energy is not fully defined, scientists have measured increased photon emissions and electromagnetic readings about healers who emit it during their work.

Emotional energy is contagious. It can make the difference between a toxic and healthy relationship. It is crucial to get a clear read on this aspect of anyone you plan to regularly interact with. Then, you can decide whether a relationship is feasible, based on your energetic compatibility. Forcing anything is simply the mind's attempt to interfere with the flow. Of course, we all have anxieties, fears, but energy cements our bond with others and motivates us to work through the rough spots. Nevertheless, healthy relationships have a momentum that carries them, a surrender that feels more natural when you are both in sync. Ultimately, the energy transmitted by someone's smile and presence tells the truth about where they are at. So, it is good to correlate a person 's energy with their emotions.

Our Vibration Frequency Code is based on an overall accumulation of emotions, our attitude and how we respond and react. How long and intense that we stay in certain thoughts and emotions that generate feelings is what actualizes and expands the accumulated energy of consciousness that becomes our vibrational frequency.

Table 2 gives a list of energy levels for various emotions taken from Dr. David R. Hawkin's book, *Power vs Force*.[18] Kinesiology is based on testing of an all-or-none muscle response to stimuli. A positive stimulus provokes a strong muscle response; a negative stimulus results in a demonstrable weakening of the test muscle.

Moreover, he found that this testable phenomenon can be used to calibrate human levels of consciousness so that an arbitrary logarithmic scale of whole numbers emerges, stratifying the relative power of levels of consciousness in all areas of human experience. According to him, exhaustive investigation has resulted in a calibrated scale of consciousness, in which the log of whole numbers from 1 to 1,000 calibrates the degree of power of all possible levels of human awareness. In his book, he also describes each one in detail.

- Shame ... energy level 20
- Guilt ... energy level 30
- Apathy ...energy level 50
- Grief ...energy level 75
- Fear ... energy level 100
- Desire ... energy level 125
- Anger ... energy level 150
- Pride ... energy level 175
- Courage ... energy level 200
- Neutrality ... energy level 250
- Willingness ... energy level 310

- Acceptance ... energy level 350

- Reason ... energy level 400

- Love ... energy level 500

- Joy ... energy level 540

- Peace ... energy level 600

- Enlightenment ... energy level 700 - 1000

Table 2: Energy levels of various emotions

Looking at the list above, we can clearly see that the lower energy levels of negative energy can really weigh us down. When we look at how the energy levels progress higher, as we emotionalize love, joy, peace and enlightenment really tips the scale. Our body absorbs whatever emotion we are feeling. So, if we are angry most of the day, we are energizing low energy that will create us to be fatigued and listless as we have no energy, and prolonged low energy eventually sinks into depression and hopelessness.

When it is said that someone is "possessed," what is meant is that his consciousness has become dominated by negative attractor fields from which the person cannot extricate himself.

## Hyper-Communication at the Cellular Level[19]

Only 10% of our DNA is being used for building proteins. This suggests that the 90% of human DNA which is not involved in protein building is active within a quantum state. If human consciousness begins to shift its vibratory rate, as a reaction to various external impacts (cosmic, environmental, cultural), then there is every likelihood that DNA will likewise show a resonance shift.

The Russian biophysicist and molecular biologist Pjotr Garjajev, who has studied human DNA with his research team in Moscow, has found that the 90% 'inactive' DNA actually has complex properties. Garjajev discovered that the DNA which is not used for protein synthesis is, instead, actually used for communication, more exactly – for hyper-communication. In their terms, hyper-communication refers to a data exchange on DNA level using genetic code. Garjajev and his group analyzed the vibration response of the DNA and concluded that it can function much like networked intelligence, and that it allows for hyper-communication of information amongst all sentient beings.

The claims of hyper-communication can be compared to the organization of ant colonies. They make use of a distributed form of communication. When a queen ant is separated from her colony, the worker ants continue to build and construct the colony as if following some form of blueprint. Yet, if the queen ant is killed, then all work in the colony ceases, as if the blueprint had suddenly been taken off-line. This suggests that the queen ant need not be in physical contact to continue to transmit the blueprint. Upon death, however, the group consciousness ceases to operate within a hyper-communicative informational field. We can thus refer to these forms of hyper-communication as quantum field consciousness, or simply as quantum consciousness.

In a similar manner, human phenomenon as remote healing, remote sensing, and telepathy may work along comparable lines. On a more basic level we could say that many of us experience this as the sense of intuition and moments of inspiration. We may even be receiving these forms of hyper-communication when we are asleep. There are countless examples of people, artists, and designers who have gained inspiration for their work in their dreams.

## Conclusion

Altered State of Consciousness has been used in many occult practices. We have seen that Pythia in Delphi gave her oracles in an Altered State of Consciousness. Hypnotic trance is an Altered State of Consciousness wherein a hypnotised person can do things which may not be possible for other people. Religious rituals can provide a condition for creating Altered States of Consciousness. We also have seen that Placebo effect is another effect of Altered State of Consciousness. The moon seems to affect some people during various phases of the moon.

Normal sight is restricted to the visible light range, in which we can see the full spectrum of colours from red to violet. Photographic film incorporates most of the normal light spectrum and extends to some degree into the ultra violet. Clairvoyants are people who, for one reason or another, can see beyond the normal range of sight. Many psychics are clairvoyant. These people are able to see a broader range of vibrations, incorporating the infra-red at the lower end and the ultra violet at the higher end of the spectrum.

Most of us are aware that other animals are able to hear at different rates of vibration, for instance, dogs can hear much higher rates of vibration than we can, and so we have the "silent" dog whistles, which they can hear, but we cannot. But do we really consider sound waves such as radar, television, and radio waves? We know they are all around us, but we need special electronic devices to pick them up - of particularly active mercury fillings, as some people have discovered! Clairaudients are psychics who have extended their hearing capacities beyond those normally found in the human species and are able to hear things the rest of us cannot.

Some people may have a special ability to sense vibrations around people and that explains their ability for mediumship. People who have high sensitivity to water and basalt may be able to sense their presence and therefore dowsing and crystal gazing may be explained. Mentally disturbed people who are vibrating at a different frequency may be able to create poltergeist phenomena.

Healing and Exorcism: Besides faith, Placebo effect, and altered states of consciousness, the healer's vibrational frequency may influence healing and exorcism.

The discussion on Altered States of Consciousness shows that occult experiences have a deep connection with ASCs. Is it a necessary condition for occult phenomena is a question to be resolved.

## Endnotes

[1] Wikipedia, the free encyclopedia, "Mind," (accessed 29 January, 2016), https://en.wikipedia.org/wiki/Mind

[2] Ludwig Arnold, JAMA Psychiatry, 1966;15(3):225-234

[3] James William, Varieties of religious experience, Longmanns, Green & Co, New York, 1929, pp.378-379

[4] Arnold M. Ludwig, "Altered States of Consciousness" in Charles Tart, ed., *Altered States of Consciousness* (Garden City, NY: Doubleday/ Anchor, 1972), p.16

[5] John White, ed., *What Is Enlightenment?: Exploring the Goal of the Spiritual Path*, Los Angeles, CA: J. P. Tarcher, 1984, p.xiii

[6] Fox, J. (1803). *A new medical dictionary*. London: Darton and Harvey

[7] Malani, A. 2006, "Identifying placebo effects with data from clinical trials. *Journal of Political Economy*, vol. 114, no. 2, pp.236-256

[8] Giordano, J. 2008, "Placebo and placebo effects: "Practical considerations, ethical concerns", *American Family Physician,* vol. 77, no. 9,1316-1318, p.1316

[9] Colloca, L., & Benedetti, F. 2005, "Placebos and painkillers: Is mind as real as matter?", *Neuroscience,* vol. 6, pp.545-552

[10] Moerman, D. 2002. *Meaning, Medicine, and the "Placebo Effect",* University Press, Cambridge, UK

[11] Wampold, B. E., Minami, T., Callen Tierney, S., Baskin, T. W., & Bhati, K. S. 2005, "The placebo is powerful: Estimating placebo effects in medicine and psychotherapy from randomized clinical trials", *Journal of Clinical Psychology,* vol. 61, no. 7, pp.835-854

[12] Kaptchuk, T. J. 2002. "The placebo effect in alternative medicine: Can the performance of a healing ritual have clinical significance?", *Annals of Internal Medicine,* vol.136, pp.817-825

# Chapter 3

# Occult and Supernatural Phenomena in the Bible

## The Occult and Supernatural Phenomena in the Old Testament

The Bible is a mine of information on paranormal phenomena. Nearly every book of the Bible shows the belief that human beings have contact with more than just the physical world and that there are other ways of influencing the world and people than physical means. Divination and works of power are found throughout the Bible. There is even discussion on what kind of practices are forbidden and why.

In the Old Testament we can find traces of magic and other occult practices. The biblical tradition is adamant against the profusion of occult that enveloped their tiny Israelite kingdom. While bits and pieces of magic entered their religious life, the highest religious tradition of Israel never felt comfortable with them. During the long history of Israelite religion, elements of occult practices continued, and they are frankly recorded in the Bible. Sometimes, the occult practices receive merciless condemnation, and other times they slip into the accepted faith unnoticed.

## Condemnation of the Occult in the Old Testament

The passages condemning the occult practices are:

1. Dt 18:9-14. In this passage, nine kinds of occult practices are condemned.

2. 2 Kings 21:2-6. In this passage we have an account of occult practices that King Manasseh indulged in.

3. 1 Chron 10:13-14. King Saul had lost the battle and was killed by the Philistines on Mount Gilboa due to his consulting the medium, the witch of Endor.

4. Lev 19:31; 20:6; 20:27. In these passages, consulting medium is banned.

5. Is 8:9-20. Isaiah condemns all those who consult medium and wizards.

6. Exo 22:18. In this passage, there is a command not to allow sorceress to live.

7. Lev 19:26.This verse is a command not to practice augury or witchcraft.

8. Is 2:6. In this passage, the prophet Isaiah says that God has rejected the house of Jacob because they are full of diviners and soothsayers.

9. 9 Jer. 27:9-10. In this passage, Jeremiah advises the kings not to listen to the  soothsayers, sorcerers and diviners.

If these condemnations are taken out of context, the conclusion is that every capacity for paranormal experience must come from the Devil unless there is proof that it is a gift from God. Turning to the occult is a turning away from God. God himself can use these ways of communicating, but the initiative must be entirely on his part. The fact that training may be needed to hear the voice of God is never mentioned.

Of all the passages, the most exhaustive list of the multiple forms of occult is found in the book of Deuteronomy.

## *The Deuteronomic Condemnation of the Occult Practices*

The Deuteronomic laws are believed to have been complied in the middle of the 7th century B.C in the northern kingdom. These laws, no doubt, reflect a much older usage and the Exodus laws would appear to represent that usage. These condemnations in the Deuteronomic code show that the Israelites were practicing polytheistic cults.

These laws are a response to a real situation. Otherwise, such laws would have had no relevance. We must take note also of the fact that the prophets were individuals, unlike the priests who served in guilds and carried out the cultic practices. The prophets, therefore, were not considered as the priests were as an institution. The ministry of the prophets was from the heart.

There were prophets speaking out for the worship of Canaanite gods, and at the same time, there were Israelite prophets speaking for the worship of Yahweh. Here is a passage which illustrates this: "If a prophet rises among you or a dreamer of dreams and gives you a sign of a wonder… and if he says, 'let us go after other gods which you have not known and let us serve them; you shall not listen."[1] The most striking evidence of the contest between the two kinds of prophets is to be found in the remarkable story of Elijah and the prophets of Baal in 1 Kings 18:20. Another kind of anti- Canaanite legislations in the book of Deuteronomy is 'You shall not cut yourselves to make any baldness on your foreheads for the dead.' The cult of the dead was an advanced and sophisticated one in Egypt and the Israelites knew of it. Jacob, father of Israel was after all mummified[2]. The Deuteronomic condemnations are set within a wider context of idealized history, retrojected to a time before the entry into Canaan was achieved. In other words, the Deuteronomist is telling the people that they must, on no account, do these occult practices, if Yahweh is to lead and protect them in their new world..

The passage we are examining (Dt 18: 9-11) is given below:

> When you come into the land which the Lord your God gives you, you shall not learn to follow the abominable practices of those nations. There shall not be found among you anyone who burns his son or daughter as an offering anyone who practices divination, a soothsayer, or an augur or a sorcerer. Or a charmer, or a medium or a wizard or a necromancer. For whoever does these things is an abomination to the Lord, and because of these abominable practices the Lord your God is driving them out before you. You shall be blameless before the Lord your God.

Verse 9 sets the pattern by condemning the pagan practices of other nations. The nations concerned are primarily the Canaanite kingdoms of Ugarit southwards, through Egypt and Mesopotamia whose influences on Canaan must not be forgotten. Verses 10 and 11 contain details of the sort of pagan practices that would separate a believer from God. Verse 12 makes it clear that the service of the Lord requires utter devotion to him and this is made explicit in the well known terms of the prophetic movement.

We are interested in verses 10 and 11. Aside from the first reference to the sacrifice of a son or a daughter, which is probably a unique Canaanite practice, it is a specific reference to the custom of sacrificing a son or a daughter to Molech, the Ammonite version of Baal. We find in Leviticus condemnation of this practice:[3] "You shall not give any of your children to devote them by fire to Molech and so profane the name of your God." We read in the book of Kings how King Josiah dealt with such customs: "And he defiled Topheth, which is in the valley of the sons of Hinnom, that no one might burn his son or his daughter as an offering to Molech."[4]

The cultic practitioners condemned are specialists listed in three categories. There are three types of diviners – augur, soothsayer, and diviner; two types of malevolent magicians – sorcerer and caster of spells; and three types of specialist spiritists. The various translations of the Bible use various terms for them.

## a.    *The Three Types of Diviners*

### 1.    *Anyone who Practices Divination*

This type of divining concerns the drawing of lots. What probably happened was that headless arrows would be inscribed with a word, placed in a quiver or another container, whirled around or shaken, and the first arrow to fall out would be the divinely chosen one. Thus, the God's will had been expressed. We also learn that the Mesopotamians of Biblical times also used this means of discovering God's will for in Ez 21:19 we are told that the Babylonian King, Nebuchadnezzar, stood at the junction of the roads to Jerusalem and Rabbah in Ammon. In order to decide which road to take he sought God's will by shaking the arrows back and forth and by holding in his right hand the arrow indicating the Jerusalem road. Thus, this term indicates a method of divining the will of the deity by means of headless 'cut' arrows.

## 2.    *Soothsayer*

This word occurs in Judges 9:37 where we read of 'the oak of the soothsayers.' It would seem from this that soothsayers had a special place near an oak tree, where they practiced their art and were available for consultation.

## 3.    *Augur*

Augur can relate to 'hissing noises.' But we must admit that a word may lose its original meaning through centuries of cult practice, so that the final meaning seems little connected with the root meaning. For instance, in Genesis 44:4, Joseph said 'why have you stolen my silver cup?' In the next verse it is asked, 'Is it not from this that my Lord drinks and by this that he divines?' We may well ask what form of divining is achieved from a silver cup. Was it from the sound of the liquid being poured in, the liquid itself, or the dregs? Or perhaps, there was a froth which made a hissing noise. If Joseph indeed practiced divination by means of a silver cup, then he could have been practicing hydromancy or watching the play of light on the liquid.

We can conclude that this has to do with some sound made by diviners; therefore, we may suppose that it is related with the cultic muttering or whispering of oracular statements divined by the augur perhaps in a state of trance.

## b.    *The Two Types of Magicians*

## 1.    *Sorcerer*

The Hebrews knew of the Egyptian sorcerers as in Exodus 9:11. Pharaoh summoned the wise men and the sorcerers, and the Egyptians too, did the same thing by their spells.

The prophets saw the 'sorcerers' as living sources of seductive and corruptive influences; e.g. Jezebel[5] or the great Assyrian city of Nineveh.[6] If the Exodus law should demand the death of a sorcerer as in Exod 22:18, it is proof enough that the Israelites were subject to the influences of magical pagan practices. The worship of Yahweh, who alone did wonders, needed no magic.

## 2. *Charmer*

The root word for a charmer in Hebrew is <u>Hābēr, which</u> means both 'company' and 'spell.' One illustration of its meaning is given in Psalm 58:5: "and [they] will not listen to the sound of the charmer, however sinful his spells may be.

Babylonia was famed throughout the ancient world for its magic and Isaiah 47:9 reflects this: "For all your monstrous sorceries, your countless spells perish in your spells and your monstrous sorceries with which you have trafficked all your life." Thus, this double term clearly has to do with binding people by spells. The prophets wanted the people to be Yahweh-bound and they bitterly condemned such magical practices which lured the ordinary people away from the true path.

## c. *The Three Types of Specialist Spiritists*

This last group are 'those who traffic with ghosts and spirits'

## 1. *Medium*

There seems to be a clear connection in terms of the Hebrew view of the dead in their shadowy, vague and formless life in the underworld with the famous 'witch of Endor,' whose story is given in 1 Sam 28:7. She could call dead person's spirit. So shō'el 'ôböt must mean 'one who makes enquiry of ghosts or spirits from the underworld. Just as one asks someone something or in a sense 'calls him to his attention,' so the practitioner calls upon the ghosts (shades of the dead) and there must be an element of interrogation implied. So, the practitioner is one who was believed to be able to summon up the shades of the dead.

## 2.    *Wizard*

It is a noun from the ordinary Hebrew verb for 'to know'. Therefore, it is 'one who knows' in some very special way. This word occurs in the context which makes it clear that 'this knowing' one is the one who has special knowledge of the underworld. He knows about ghosts; he has intimate and secret knowledge of them. He can contact them.

## 3.    *Necromancer*

The phrase literally means 'one who seeks the dead' and in a way parallels the previous two terms. There is ancient Egyptian evidence for the practice of going to the tomb of one's beloved and speaking to them, admitting past guilt, seeking favour, and so on. This we find in Is 65:4 'crouching among graves, keeping vigil all night long, eating swine's flesh, and their cauldrons full of tainted brew.' Certainly, it is a primitive mourning custom which involves the calling of the dead.

The list of nine kinds of condemned occult practices is now complete. overall, we are not left in much doubt as to the nature of the practices involved. What is clear is that the Israelites from the earliest times were involved in these. They were age-old practices inherited by the Israelites. The ordinary people may have been expected to indulge in them but that even the highest authorities in the land did so is an indication of the all-pervasive influence of Canaanite religion throughout the land of Israel.

Though King Saul issued an edict against consulting 'women with familiar spirits' echoing the Deuteronomic tradition, he violated this himself by consulting the prophet Samuel through the 'witch of Endor' in his moment of supreme need. This incident at least illustrates the point that the Israelites believed in the possibility of 'spirit contacts' but had forbidden them for other reasons than disbelief in medium as an effective technology. The Israelites lived in an environment in which such things as magic and medium or contacts with 'gods' and spirits were phenomena universally taken for granted. Thus, the Dueteronomic condemnation of occult practices was a necessity to protect the infant Israelite religion from being swallowed up by conflicting revelations, doctrines, and values which came through the mouths of different oracles, prophets, and priests, all claiming inspiration by different gods or spirits.

## The Accepted Occult Practices of Israel

We find that certain occult practices were fostered or allowed in the Old Testament. Some of these, in some way, predict the future, change the course of events in the future and communicate with a non-worldly realm. Now, we shall investigate those practices which are normally accepted as good.

### 1.  *The Magical Approach to Life in Israel*

In Canaanite Israel, the magical approach was primarily shaped by the Canaanite vegetation and fertility cults, whose basis was largely magical. In the magical world view, one expects to strengthen the deity and maintain the mysterious forces of life by means of sexual rites or to reawaken the rhythm of nature each year and render the earth fertile through rites centering on a deity that fades away and then revives. The Israelites adopted many Canaanite magical practices. They had also brought others along out of their own nomadic past. Some of these magical practices mentioned in the Old Testament are:

- Magical use of a staff: Moses used his staff to work miracles in front of the Pharaoh in Egypt[7].

- Magical use of clothing as in the case of Elisha. The prophet Elijah went to meet Elisha and threw his mantle over his shoulders and Elisha received power.[8]

- Belief in the magical power of outstretched hand as in the case of Naaman getting angry because the prophet Elisha did not wave his hand over him[9].

- Effective magic word, whether spoken as blessing or curse by an ordinary man especially at the hour of death. Jacob through deceit got the blessing of Isaac but when Esau came and begged his father to bless him also, he said whatever he has done cannot be reversed.[10]

- Joshua 10:12 is an example of the power of word by a leader filled with supernatural power. Joshua made the Sun stand still so that the Israelites could defeat the Amorites.

- Deborah is reported to have sung a magical war song, paving the way for the defeat of the enemy.[11]

- It is reasonable to suppose that the concept of prophetism in 1 and 2 Kings with its belief in the almost magical power of the 'men of God' and prophetical leaders is a remnant of that primitive culture in which the various functions still combined in a single person. The magical element of the early period continues in the notion of effective power of prophetic words and actions. This notion pervaded all Israelite prophecy where it is based on the will and the power of Yahweh.

- Even some of the legends found in the Old Testament material reflect certain belief in magical practices. Otherwise they would not have been put in writing. A woman might seek by their aid to overcome her husband's aversion: "When Jacob came from the field in the evening, Leah went out to meet him, and said. "You must come into me; for I have hired you with my son's mandrakes."[12]

- A herdsman might seek to influence the litter of his sheep: "Then Jacob took fresh rods of poplar and almond and plane, and peeled white streaks in them, exposing the white of the rods. He set the rods which he had peeled in front of the flocks in the runnels, that is, the watering troughs, where the flocks came to drink. And since they bred when they came to drink, the flocks bred in front of the rods and so the flocks brought forth striped, speckled and spotted."[13]

- Harmful springs were to be made wholesome by means of salt and poisonous food by means of 'meal': "Then he went to the spring of water and threw salt in it, and said, 'Thus says the Lord, I have made this water wholesome; henceforth neither death nor miscarriage shall come from it.'[14] "But while they were eating of the pottage, they cried out, 'O man of God, there is death in the pot'. And they could not eat it. Elisha said, "Then bring meal" and he threw it into the pot and said, "Pour out for the men that they may eat. And there was no harm in the pot."[15]

- Men interpreted dreams and constellations: Prophet Jeremiah warns the Israelites: "Learn not the way of the nations, nor be dismayed at the signs of the heaven."[16] And the book of Deuteronomy warns the people not to believe the miraculous claims of magicians in these words:

If a prophet arises among you, or a dreamer of dreams and gives you a sign or a wonder, and the sign or wonder which he tells you comes to pass, and if he says 'Let us go after other gods, which you have not known and let us serve them, you shall not listen to the words of that prophet or to that dreamer of dreams.[17]

There was the practice of observing bubbles and refraction for predicting the future: "Is it not from this that my Lord drinks, and by this that he divines?" as given in the Book of Genesis about Joseph.[18] In order to know the future, either arrows were drawn from a receptacle shaken well, or the livers of sacrificial animals examined for colour and shape as narrated in the book of Ezekiel by the King of Babylon:"For the king of Babylon stands at the parting of the way, at the head of the two ways, to use divination; he shakes the arrows, he consults the teraphim, he looks at the liver."[19] Though the king of Babylon is doing this, it looks as though it is an accepted practice among the Israelites. In this way, people thought they could recognize, influence or control the great forces of life in order to be masters of their own lives, protect themselves against evil and make the most of their existence. With the notion of Yahweh as the God of heaven is linked to that of figures belonging to the heavenly world, called divine beings. These heavenly beings were usually sent forth to carry out Yahweh's bidding. At a sacred spot, a man may see in a dream how they go up and down a stairway connecting heaven and earth as in the case of Jacob at Bethel.[20]

There is frequent mention of the phrase mal'āk Yhwk, the angel of the Lord. This messenger appears as a bearer of revelation and of aid. An angel rescues Hagar as she flees from Sarai;[21] an angel announces the birth of Samson.[22] An angel fortifies Elijah[23] and vanquishes the Assyrian army.[24] In other instances, the angel carries out on earth the will of the supreme God. Thus he is appointed to bring the Israelites safely to Palestine[25]; the angel appears to Joshua as leader of the heavenly army[26]; he calls down curses on those that have not come to Yahweh's aid in Jud 5:23 and he designates those that are to be spared by the heavenly beings following him in Exod 9:2. Among their duties may be the protection and preservation of men.[27] But they can also come as angels of destruction.[28] More humble services were assigned to the Cherubim and Seraphim. On the one hand, the Cherubim were thought of as throne bearers or a personification of thunder-clouds from which lightening can blaze forth as given in Gen 3:24. On the other hand, they appear in Ezekiel 1 and 10 as beings of mixed human and animal nature, such as are familiar primarily from Babylonian representations. The Seraphim mentioned in Isaiah 6 are similar hybrids: they have human voices, hands and faces, but also wings and a serpentine body.[29]

Belief in demons was essentially alien to true Israelite religion. Impressed by the notion of Yahweh's uniqueness, it refused to recognize any other powers. Mysterious, awful and horrifying phenomena were incorporated into the picture of God himself, or else were associated with a heavenly being or spirit sent by Yahweh. In consequence Yahweh took on 'demonic' features.[30] Demons, therefore, are seldom mentioned. It was forbidden to offer them sacrifice as given in Lev 17:7 and relations with them were prohibited, without any denial of their existence. But for many in Israel, demons symbolized the mysterious aspect of the world. They surely played an important role in popular religion. Ruins and waste places, felt to be sinister, were thought of as their dwelling places. Foreign gods, relegated to an inferior position, were counted among them. And demons from other religions invaded the Israelite conceptual world. Many of these notions finally took such firm root that they could not be eliminated but could only be reinterpreted within the framework of Yahwism.

The most important demons mentioned in the Old Testament are:

(1) Hairy demons in the form of goats, inhabiting the open countryside.[31]

(2) Black demons, i.e. sinister demons, probably former pagan gods.[32]

(3) The dry demons inhabiting waterless regions,[33] the desert animals mentioned in the same context are probably conceived as demons in animal form.

(4) Azazel, a demon lying in the desert, who was thought to receive the scapegoat released in the ceremony of the great Day of Atonement as given in Lev 16.

(5) Demons bringing sickness, striking by day or night, as given in Ps 91:5-6.

(6) Lilith, by origin probably an Assyrian storm demon, then considered a nocturnal demon, because of the similarity to the Hebrew word for 'light' as given in Is 34:14.

Like the Canaanites, the Israelites sensed the presence of demons everywhere —not only in the desert, so that an annual sacrifice to one of them seemed necessary as given in Lev 16 but also in the settled territory where the fertility of the fields, the security of the house and the health of people depended, at least in part, on them. There were men and women skilled in the dangerous techniques of gaining influence over such powers or rendering them subservient. They could exorcise diseases, impose or release a spell, bring about unlucky days, make rain, and practice necromancy. The people were probably more devoted to magic than is usually assumed. People feared the perpetual threat of demons and the magical powers of their neighbours. They, therefore, performed magical actions to protect themselves and injure their foes. In many psalms, we can still catch echoes of the notion that the disaster afflicting a person is due to a spell that must be broken by a counter-spell. Excavations, too, have brought various magical devices to light: execration tablets containing curses upon the enemy; small figurines with hands and feet bound, intended to bind the enemy through imprisonment, sickness or death; numerous amulets like blue pearls against the evil eye, small silver hands for the protection of children, and symbols of gods or demons to assure their patronage.

## 2.   Oracles and Divination

Like all peoples of antiquity, the Jewish people were always trying to discover future events, the result of an enterprise or some secret things by questioning God. Many and varied are the ways of obtaining an oracle an answer from God. But those who try to wrest a secret from the divinity, those who consult the dead or other gods are condemned. Therefore, the Old Testament makes a very sharp distinction between legitimate prophecies, either cultic or private, and the cultic prophecies of the neighbouring peoples and popular divination.

Much of the cult of the people was tainted with magic. The diviner pronounced his oracle by his own power, by his higher intuition, by his art, or using objects or rites which men held to be infallible or capable of constraining gods or demons. On the contrary, the Israelite priest and prophet knew that no oracle could be obtained unless Yahweh consented. The Jewish people knew that they depended on his God; when they questioned Yahweh, they awaited an answer from His goodness and kindness; they did not try to wrest it from Him; they asked for it,[34] for Yahweh does not allow Himself to be constrained and can refuse an answer.[35] The prophets especially express this sentiment. For example, when they compare themselves to watchmen as in Is 21:6,8, or are on the look-out for God's word as in Ez 3:16-17; 33:7, or when they pray to obtain a favour as in Jer 42:4.

## 3.    *Sacerdotal Oracle*

The sacerdotal oracle is pronounced by a priest. To pronounce an oracle is one of the priest's principal functions as seen in Dt 33:8. Moses had earlier issued oracles to those 'who were seeking Yahweh' in 'the meeting tent,'[36] in the Sanctuary, where Yahweh met Moses and spoke to him. He settled the differences of those who came 'to consult God' and 'made known God's decrees and decisions. Likewise, according to Dt 17:18-12, serious lawsuits had to be taken in the sanctuary before the Levitical priests, whose sentence had to be accepted without qualification under the pain of death. Beginning with the period of the Judges, there are many examples of oracles given by priests.[37] On many occasions Saul and David consulted God through the meditation of the priest.[38] The priest questioned Yahweh by the 'urîm and the tummîm, as seen in Dt 33:8. The meaning of these words, the nature, form and use of these objects are not known. According to Ex 28:30, Lev 8:8, Num 27:21, these objects were kept in the container affixed to the 'ephod which rested on the high priest's chest. It was a lot. In Israel the sacred lot was served to make known Yahweh's decisions.[39]. Consulting Yahweh by urîm and the tummîm_is no longer mentioned after the age of David.[40] Nehemiah 7:65 shows that this method was no longer the custom after the Exile. The terāpîm were associated in several places with the ephod[41]_and are also cult objects used in securing oracles[42] in the national cult and in private homes.[43] It is not known how oracles were given by the terāpîm. In several texts they are condemned as cult objects of foreign origin[44] or tainted with superstition.[45] They were excluded from official worship at the time of the Deuteronomy reform. Yet they did not disappear completely from popular religion.[46]

## 4.    *Private Foretelling*

Abraham's servant asks Yahweh to show a sign, which young girl is destined to become the wife of this master's son. The sign he had selected was that a young girl would give him a drink of water and then would give water to his camels. This girl did and revealed Yahweh's choice as seen in Gen 24:12-27. In the same way Jonathan specified the sign by which he would know whether Yahweh would grant him a victory over the Philistines. He decided that if the Philistine guard, when seeing them would invite them to advance toward them, Yahweh would make him victorious. But if the guard ordered the two men to halt, then the Israelites would be defeated. When the first hypothesis was fulfilled, Jonathan, followed by his servant, attacked them and slaughtered many in the enemy's camp as given in 1 Sam 14:8-15. Sometimes a chance happening was interpreted as a sign from Yahweh[47] because they felt that nothing takes place unless Yahweh has so willed and arranged.[48]

Another form of popular divination consisted in obtaining oracles from trees, especially from sacred trees, whose murmuring was interpreted as a divine response as seen in 2

Sam 5:24 and the oak of the diviners seen in Jud 9:37. Worship
given to these sacred trees was condemned by the prophets as
given in Is 1:29. Like most of the ancient people, the Hebrews
admitted that in dreams God communicated to His servants
knowledge of the future[49] or warnings[50] or the revelation of
things unknown as in Gen 28:12-15. According to Num 12:6,
dreams and visions were the usual means in which God revealed
himself to the prophets. In fact, Dt 13:2 considered prophets
to be synonymous with dreamers. Yet, if the great prophets
spoke frequently of their visions, they did not seem to make
much of their dreams.[51] Despite the belief in the value of the
symbolic dream, a science of dream interpretation failed to
develop among the Hebrews. Biblical religion preferred that
form of dream and vision which suited best its aspiration to
get God above all. It is Yahweh who causes dreams and it is
he who provides an explanation of their meaning.

## 5.    *Ecstasy and Prophecy*

The highest form of Israelite prophecy – the apostle of prophecy
– is a peculiarly Hebrew conception. But Hebrew prophecy
contains ancient pagan elements that have been refashioned
by the Hebrew conception. All forms of Hebrew prophecy
contained altered states of consciousness. For example, the
seventy elders who stand about the tent when God speaks
with Moses are seized with the spirit and 'prophecy' together
as given in Num 11:16. In Samuel's time, there is a popular
movement of the ecstatic: Gibeah has its 'band of prophets' who
prophesy to the accompaniment of psaltery, timbrels and pipes.
The elation is contagious. When Saul meets them, he is seized
and 'prophesizes' with them. Ramah has a band of 'prophets'
over whom Samuel presides. Saul's messengers, upon coming
to Ramah and even Saul himself are overcome by their frenzy,

as given in 1 Sam 10:5. In every age, Israelite prophecy displays characteristic signs of ecstasy. An extraordinary inner tension seizes the prophet; all his experiences become heightened and his spirit and body are abnormally moved. He senses himself impelled by an external power – the hand of Yahweh. In this state, he may perform extraordinary feats of physical prowess as seen in 1 Kings 18:47 or live alone 'filled with indignation' as in the case of Jeremiah in Jer 15:17 or fall prostrate.[52] At times the ecstasy takes the form of paralysis and dumbness as given in Ez 3:26. Fear and deep sleep overwhelm him as given in Dan 8:17, and his aspect changes, pains seize him; his strength and breath leave him as given in Dan 10:8, 16. Ezekiel hears the tumult and rumble of earthquakes in Ez 1:24. He feels himself borne on the wind from place to place in Ez 3:12; 14:8-11; 37:1. And yet there is an essential distinction between the Hebrew and Pagan conceptions of prophecy. Pagan prophecy is typically regarded as deriving from a specific source of occult power – from a psychic gift of the prophet, natural or acquired or from substances or spirits that inspire him. The Hebrew conception knows no such specific power sources, nor are there specific spiritual beings whose function it is to inspire. No prophet of Israel has a special sense for discerning the unknown. In fact, the Bible almost goes out of its way to emphasize that prophecy is not a native faculty. Prophecy is therefore not regarded as a native talent. The prophetic spirit is not in the prophet but 'comes upon him'.

## 6.   *Leaders Endowed with Psychic Powers*

The history of Israel begins when Abraham listened to a voice speaking within him to leave Ur of the Chaldeans and go to a new land. There he was given a vision of the fire passed between the pieces of a sacrifice as the pledge of

God's being with him. These Jewish patriarchs were sensitive to intrusions from beyond the space-time world and directed their lives by them. The young Jacob was given the same kind of encouragement when he was fleeing from his brother, Esau. In his sleep he saw a ladder ascending to heaven, and from above, God gave Jacob the same pledge he had made to Abraham. The meaning of Joseph's life revolved around his remembering and interpreting dreams. This accounted for his being sold into slavery and then for his release from prison and his rise to power. When he was asked about his ability to interpret dreams, Joseph replied: "Do not interpretations belong to God?" There was nothing wrong with divining dreams, unless one did it falsely or for one's own gain. Moses, it has been recorded, met God face to face. He had no need for difficult and uncertain divination. Yahweh spoke to other men, even to prophets, in dreams, which they had to struggle hard to understand. Experiencing the bush which burned but not consumed, Moses was transformed by God into a better wizard than any of the Egyptian sorcerers so that he could lead his people out of Egypt.

For Samuel, the choice of God came in the night, but he had to be instructed to listen and respond. Later, Samuel did not have to search for Saul to make him king over Israel. Saul came to Samuel for help through his clairvoyant ability, for he knew that his father's asses were lost. Samuel knew what had happened to the asses and he knew that this was the young man of whom God had spoken to him. Elijah and Elisha were open to the same kind of power. Elijah was fed by a raven. Elisha saw him carried up to heaven in a chariot of fire and he received Elijah's cloak. Later Elisha healed Naaman of his leprosy by a ritual washing and gave him some Israelite soil to take home so that he could worship Yahweh properly there. He opened Gehazi's eyes so that he could see the multitude of angels surrounding them. He also made an axe head float in water in a most unscientific way. Elijah took on the prophets of Baal who lived on Mt. Carmel in a duel of magic and wonder-working to see who had more power to work wonders as they are the necessary conditions of an authentic divinity. The Elijah/Elisha cycle contains several occult elements, including passing on a power-giving mantle from Elijah to the apprentice Elisha and healing people through personal rituals. Elisha had already denounced Jezebel, the daughter of the king of Tyre and a follower of Baal and prophesied her horrible death in 2 Kings 9:10. Thus ended a long feud between Jezebel, representing the power of Baal and Elisha, representing the power of Yahweh. The activities engaged in by both sides of this struggle seem quite alike to us. The difference, of course, depends on whose magic you are offering, Baal's or Yahweh's. By the time of the 8th century prophets, the distinction between true and false prophets took on a more ethical quality. Belomancy or the use of arrows for advice, provided the mortally ill Elisha with the word of victory sought by his client, King Jehoash. But the king, who had to do the ritualistic procedures himself because Elisha lay on his deathbed, did not follow the ritual properly and thus could only be sure of a partial victory over the enemy, Aram.[53] Even in death, Elisha retained the magical powers Elijah had given to him. When some people unknowingly threw a body into his grave, after a Moabite guerrilla raid, the deceased touched the prophet's bones and the" man came to life and rose to his feet."[54]

## 7.   Symbols Endowed with Power

In its earliest stages, magic and ritual in Israel are too closely intertwined. We read taboos and spells, such as in Judges 5:21-24: "A curse on Meroz, said the angel of the Lord; A curse, a curse on its inhabitants, because they brought no help to the Lord."

The people used holy water to cleanse someone who had touched the dead. The ashes from the sin-offering, and marjoram, were sprinkled over the unclean person according to a specific ritual.[55] The institution of the so-called scapegoat offering[56] also reflects magical practices. Aaron, the priest, was to cast lots over the two goats, choosing one for the Lord and the other for Azazel, the wilderness demon. The second goat wasn't sacrificed on the altar but rather loaded with the sins of the people and driven away 'into the wildernesses to a precipice, over which it would fall and somehow rid the Israelite society of influences of dark power. Blood sprinkling and sacrifices to invite Yahweh's presence among the people are only a few more of the magical elements in Israelite religion. To this list, we can add the holy places, such as Shechem, which Joshua chose to enhance the authority of hi s covenant renewal ceremony, and Shiloh where the ark once rested and Samuel saw the Lord.[57] The bells which Aaron put on his priestly robes represent more magical elements, so the"sound of it shall be heard when he enters the Holy Place before the Lord and when he comes out; and so he shall not die."[58]

## The Occult and Supernatural Phenomena in the Gospels

The gospels record several occult phenomena. The birth of Jesus was announced in a dream to Joseph.[59] Jesus performed many healing miracles, and exorcised demons[60] although he declared definitely that his power was not from Satan.[61] His method did not stress the action involved in healing, but emphasized the faith of the cured one:" Your faith has made you well." Preparing for his ministry Jesus went out into the wilderness and was beset with visions of satanic temptation.[62] One supernatural experience which the Gospels record is hard to dismiss, because theologically, it is central to Christian doctrine: The Resurrection of Jesus Christ. Paranormal phenomena in the ministry of Jesus exist on record, whether modern Christians feel comfortable with them or not.

When we see the large numbers of miraculous phenomena cited in the gospels, we cannot simply avoid taking them into consideration. Jesus walked on water. He healed the sick and exorcised demons. He knew the future. He calmed the storm, read minds, practiced clairvoyance and finally arose from the dead. He was trying to destroy the evil forces. One can hardly understand his ministry, or even something as basic as the Lord Prayer, without an understanding of Jesus in battle against the forces of evil. Jesus not only used these powers himself, but he passed the same powers of superhuman knowledge, healing and exorcism to his followers. Jesus bestowed his followers with a new power that would enable them to spread the gospel effectively by using capacities that are out of the ordinary.

## 1.   *Jesus and Healing*

The gospels are filled with the healing miracles of Jesus that one cannot discount them without discounting the historicity of Jesus himself. In the first chapter of the gospel of Mark, the ministry of Jesus is characterized as threefold – a ministry of preaching, teaching and healing. Nearly one-fifth of the entire gospels are devoted to Jesus' healing and the discussions occasioned by it. Except for miracles in general, this is by far the greatest emphasis given to any one kind of experience in the narrative. We find that everywhere Jesus went; he functioned as a religious healer. There are 72 accounts, including duplications, in the four gospels, 41 distinct instances of physical and mental healing are recorded, (in all,), although they, by no means, represent the total. Many of the references summarize the healings of large numbers of persons.

Out of the 3779 verses in the 4 gospels, 727 verses relate specifically to the healing of physical and mental illness and the resurrection of the dead. In addition, there are 165 verses that deal in general with eternal life, and 31 general references to miracles that include healing. It is also clear that Jesus sent his disciples out to continue this healing ministry.[63] The characteristics of Jesus' healing are rather startling. He acts as a complete master of power. He does not experiment to see if he can achieve healing. He is always described as taking power for granted. However, faith is generally required by Jesus, but probably not always, since the centurion's servant did not even know what was taking place at a distance from where he lay. Jesus heals by touch and by word, both close and at distance. His power reached out over apparent death. Power leaves him in a way that he can feel. This power is always considered secondary to the stirring up of faith, love and dedication to the kingdom.

## 2.   *Jesus and Exorcism*

The Old Testament in its concern for monotheism described angels but avoided saying much about demonic powers. It also said little about a realm with which we could communicate in addition to the physical one. The Old Testament stressed the idea that one must look only to Yahweh. Foreign deities were considered evil and Hebrews were warned not to deal with them. In the New Testament there is a change in the attitude to evil and a new understanding of evil forces. One of the characteristics of the New Testament is that we are in touch with a spiritual world containing both good and evil forces and that we had better know them and learn how to deal with them.

In the gospels, demons are powers which cause all manner of physical illness. They enter people[64]; the sick have a demon[65]; when healed the demons come out[66] or is cast out.[67] Satan appears in the New Testament in many guises.

Mark and Luke present a simple but highly dramatic exorcism as the first practical public demonstration of the powers of Jesus. The demons within the possessed men recognize Christ and the subsequent dialogues of exorcism are conducted between Jesus and the demons, the possessed person himself being unaware of what is happening. Jesus' function was to overthrow the kingdom of demons and, as stated by Mathew, to cast them into everlasting fire specifically prepared for 'the devil and his angels.'

Jesus speaks directly to the demon. Those who reject the possibility of real demons being present in these cases and prefer to see the possessed as being deranged in the modern sense, argue that Jesus was acting in something approaching the manner of the therapist. Jesus does not use prayers or rituals. Rituals and the use of objects were characteristic of exorcism of the times. But in Jesus' case, his word alone is enough to cast out the devils. This must have been largely due to his messianic charism.

## 3. *Jesus and Psycho-kinesis*

In Lk 5:1-11 Jesus oversees a miraculous catch of fish. In Mt. 8:10, Jesus stills the storm at sea. In Mt 14:22 Jesus walks on water. In Mt 21:18, Jesus curses a fig tree and it withers up. In Mt 6:30, Jesus multiplies loaves and fishes.

## 4. *Predictions of Future*

Jesus himself made some striking predictions about future. He predicted that Peter would deny him three times before the cock crowed. He predicted the destruction of Jerusalem.

## The Occult and Supernatural Phenomena in the Acts of the Apostles

The Acts of the Apostles show that almost every major decision of the apostles, almost every step in the growth of Christianity, was taken because of a dream, a vision, a prophecy, a supernatural visitation, or divination. The successor to Judas was finally elected by lots along with prayer; Paul was struck down by a vision and then healed and converted by Ananias, who was told what to do in a clairvoyant experience. Through the experience of an angel, and later a vision and some telepathic information, St. Peter's ways were changed and Cornelius and a whole group were converted. Paul began his work on European soil because of a dream. Paul had also been present at the stoning of Stephen when the dying apostle cried out that he could see the risen Lord.

The overwhelming experience of Pentecost, with the gift of supernatural languages, was followed almost immediately by the first of a series of healings. The healings included every kind that Jesus had done, from casting out demons and healing physical illness to raising the dead. St. Paul and Barnabas were even taken to be gods, after a cripple was healed in Lucanonia.

The people called them Zeus and Hermes and tried to offer them sacrifices. Handkerchiefs, aprons, or whatever had touched Paul, was tied to heal the sick. His power through Christ outstripped the abilities of the seven sons of Sceva, when they tried to use his methods for their own purposes and had to flee. When he saved a slave girl from demonic possession, Paul was taken to court by her masters for robbing them of their oracles and the profits she had brought them.

The prison doors were opened by divine intervention, not only for St. Paul and Silas whose jailer was converted by the experience, but also for St. Peter. Several times guilty people were struck down, like the pair who had joined the community knowing they had withheld some of their property. The magician Simon was so impressed by the power of the Apostles that he offered money to buy the same power, and thus his name was given to the practice of Simony, which means buying or selling of divine favours. When Simon finally realized that the power was a gift from God, he was brought to sincere repentance. A sorcerer, who tried to interfere when the proconsul of Cyprus wanted Paul to tell him about Christ, was not as lucky.

In the minds of the apostles, their wonders were far different from the usual magic, even if the miracle stories about them read like magical acts. Their powers came from God through Jesus and were totally unique. God, the supernatural divine power, can manifest himself in human life. And when God does so, he gives gifts and powers to people who are paranormal in their effect. The supernatural world enters and alters the natural world. By theological definition at least, this is quite different from magic, but it looks much like the same thing.

St. Paul became a Christian, following a vision on the Damascus road. He wrote to the Corinthians that by the Spirit of God they would have certain gifts.[68] He could pack logical discourse and learning into a passage and place it in the same bag with paranormal events such as healing and utterances, and call both the work of one spirit. He knew the excesses to which the psychic and magical could go - this very passage was written to counsel the Corinthians who were going out of balance with their addiction to glossalalia or tongues, but he hesitated to toss the baby out with the bath water. He recognized the role of the paranormal in religious experience and the useful purpose it could serve. Rather than totally denounce these manifestations, he hoped to give them a new meaning and purpose by focusing them on Christ.

In Colossians, 1:13-20, St. Paul says that all things begin and end and are brought together in the cosmic Christ, the focus and the omega-point of all creation. Such a unifying vision that bridges the distance between the alienated man and his world is what motivates many people to explore the occult. He claims that it can be found in Christ and him alone.

## Conclusion

I have demonstrated that the Bible is devoted to supernatural and occult phenomena. Sometimes, it is difficult to discern what is occult and what is supernatural or what is through the intervention of God and what is through the intervention of the devil. On the one hand, there is an explicit condemnation of occult practices and on the other hand there were accepted occult practices. It appears that some people were blessed with supernatural powers and they made use of them for God as in the case of Moses, Joseph, Daniel, etc. When the Israelites were straying away from God and adopted the magical practices of other groups, those practices were condemned. What is obvious is that supernatural powers are part of gifted people.

The challenge is to discern between what is a God-given charism and what is magic. The charisms are gifts given by God which can be used for the benefit of the community. On the other hand, it should not be used for personal gain.

## Endnotes

1. Dt 13:1-3
2. Gen 50:2-3
3. Lev 18:21
4. 2 Kings 23:10
5. 2 Kings 9:22
6. Nahum 3:4
7. Exo 7:20
8. 1Kings 19:19
9. 2 Kings 5:11
10. Gen 27:27ff; 39-40; 48:15ff
11. Jud 5:12
12. Gen 30:16
13. Gen 30:37ff
14. 2 Kings 2:21
15. 2 Kings 4:39ff
16. Jer 10:2
17. Dt 13:1-2). Kings 17:17; 2 Kings 21:6
18. Gen 44:5
19. Eze 21:26
20. Gen 28:13
21. Gen 16:7
22. Jud 13:3
23. 1 Kings 19:7
24. 2 Kings 19:35
25. Exo 23:20 ff
26. Josh 5:13
27. Ps 34:7; 91:11-12

[28] Ps 78:49 ; Exod 12:23; Sam 24:26

[29] Num 21:6; Isa 14:29; 30:6

[30] Gen 32:22-31; Exod 4:24-26

[31] Lev 17:7; Isa 13:21; 34:14; 2 Chro 11:15

[32] Dt 32:17; Ps 106:37

[33] Is 13:21; 34:14; Jer 50:39

[34] 1 Sam 14:36-42; Gen 24:12-14; Jer 42:4

[35] 1 Sam 14:36-37; 28:6; Ex 20:3

[36] Exod 33:7-11

[37] Jud 18:5-6

[38] 1Sam 14:18, 37; 22:10; 23:2,9-12; 28:6; 30:7-8

[39] 1 Sam 10:19-21; Prov 16:32; Acts 1:26

[40] 1Sam 28:6, 1Sam 30:7

[41] Jud 17:5; 18:14-20; Os 3:4

[42] Jud 17/5; 18/14-20

[43] Gen 31:19; 1 Sam 19:13

[44] Gen 35:2-4

[45] 1 Sam 15:23; Za 10:2

[46] Za 10:2

[47] 1 Sam 24:1-5; 25:18-32; 26:2-8

[48] Amos 3:6; Gen 27:20, 42:28; Exo 21:23

[49] Gen 37:5-10,40-41; Jud 7:13-14; 1 Sam 28:6,15; Dan 2:1,4:2

[50] Gen 20:3; Job 7:14

[51] Jer 23:25-27; Is 29:7-8

[52] Num 24:4; 16; Ez 1:28

[53] 2 Kings 13:14-19

[54] 2 Kings 13:21

[55] Num 19:14

[56] Lev 16:2

[57] 1 Sam 3

[58] Ex 28:35

[59] Mt 1:20

[60] Mt 8: 16

[61] Mt 12:25

[62] Mk 1:12-13

[63] Mk 6/7-13

[64] Lk 8:30

[65] Mt 11:18;Lk 7:33

[66] Mt 17:18

[67] Mt 8:31

[68] 1 Cor 12/1-13

# Chapter 4

# The Occult and the Supernatural in the Catholic Church

Christianity is rooted in the world-view of the Bible and contains marvellous stories of visions, prophecies, revelatory dreams, manifestations of God, of angelic beings and of dead saints and heroes of Israel, miraculous healings, exorcisms of evil spirits and out of the body trips into the heavenly worlds. However, systematic theology since medieval period has discouraged any point of contact with the occult and the paranormal. The fear of witchcraft and pagan worship of gods and spirits made the church allergic to any such point of contact. In order to justify its stand, the church always goes back to the Deuteronomy condemnation of the occult practices. But the condemnation of the occult practices is only a part of the Old Testament. It has been shown in Chapter 2 of this book that many psychic phenomena were well accepted and considered as gifts of God by the Israelites in the Old Testament and later by the early Church in the New Testament.

What is condemned is the magical ritual, often borrowed from Canaanite and other cults, an alternative cult to experience supernatural powers, bypassing the God of the Israelites-Yahweh. They used magical artifices handed down through centuries of folklore, and they sought an authoritative word for God from Diviners. These practices directed the people away from God because, in a way, these practices were attempts to manipulate God. For example, necromancy sought from the dead what it ought to have sought directly from God. Such uncontrolled psychical experiences are forbidden. Also, any deliberate attempt to control and use psychic power outside of a spiritual and ethical context was not allowed. Most of these pursuits are for material gains or for some other selfish motives.

In the Christian tradition, the evidence continues from the miracles of Christ, glossolalia, astral lights (tongues of flame), and other miracles worked by the Apostles and narrated in the Acts of the Apostles. St. Peter and the other disciples developed the healing gift and precognition. Jesus appeared to St. Paul in spirit form and recruited him into the new religious movement. St. Paul used psychic phenomena as the very foundation stones of the Christian church with these words in the first letter to the Corinthians: "First apostles, second prophets, third teachers, then workers of miracles, then healers, helpers, administrators, speakers in various kinds of tongues.[1]

The general attitude expressed in the New Testament would seem to be that the spiritual gifts are by-products of the 'way' and not the most important things in spiritual life. As St. Paul said: "Though I speak with the tongues of men and of angels and have not charity, I am nothing.[2] Jesus himself taught the disciples to heal the sick and to cast out demons. Nevertheless, the dictum of the scriptures "seek first the kingdom of God and all of these things will be added unto you"[3] would seem to apply to the overall religious understanding of the New Testament. St. Paul made a big list of charisms in 1Cor 12.

Once the church became a powerful worldly-institution, however, a catastrophic change took place in the official stance of the church. The kind of psychic event that had given the church the start was now looked upon with extreme suspicion, and at times, regarded as the works of the devil. Some gifted psychics became saints, others were burned as heretics and it was hard to decide which way the judgement of the Church would go.

A few great psychics survived all hazards and were remembered as radiant saints: St. Francis of Assisi with his levitations, ecstatic visions, stigmata is revered. St. Joan of the Arc, who was clairvoyant and precognitive, was declared a witch, burned at the stake at the age of nineteen, and then, five centuries later, declared a saint. St. Teresa of Avila's psychic abilities included spirit writing, levitation, materialization, and an exceptionally acute intelligence.

Modern theology, since the 16th century, has systematically warned people not to take psychic experience as related to true spiritual development. At worst, they have accused those who have had such experiences of Satanism or witchcraft. At the same time an appeal is paradoxically made to the original myths of heavenly world, a world of angels and saints, miracles, visions and prophecies, resurrection of the dead and communion of saints in heaven. Hence, there is inconsistency in theological reflection on parapsychological experiences.

The established churches have become so secular that they seem to be the last sectors of society today to encourage the belief in the supernatural. The revival of the Charismatic movement is an exception. John Kerr concludes his book, *The Mystery and the Magic of the Occult* with these words:

> The church is becoming profoundly unspiritual, even a little ashamed as a religion as such. The occult craze ought to tell the ecclesiastical powers that even though their institutions are in trouble, religion as such is once again in the mainstream. The church can begin to recover its...purely spiritual perception of reality without shame and embarrassment.[4]

The impression one gets is that the church is more interested in banishing the spirits than in testing them to see if they be of God, more concerned with getting rid of them than understanding them.

The explanations of occultism are as varied as they are numerous in the church. The materialists seek to explain it in terms of matter and its movements by a theory of "waves," the exact nature of which is not yet known. Others believe that we are dealing with reappearances of the dead, with "rebirths" or astral body. A good many Christians fall back on the devil, who is supposed in these cases to misuse human powers to deceive us. Admittedly, they try increasingly to ascribe as many of these phenomena as possible natural powers. So far, however, they do not appear to have arrived at a satisfactory explanation.

The teaching of the Church is equally far removed from either extreme, from materialism as from demon-mania. The Church does not deny the possibility of diabolical possession and even has special ordination, conferring powers of exorcism for the casting out of devils, but she enjoins us to treat everything as natural until the contrary is proved, a rule that she applies with strictness when alleged miracles are cited in the canonization process.

## Occult and Supernatural Experiences in the Lives of the Saints

The lives of saints in every period have been touched by miraculous events. St. John of the Cross was embarrassed by his tendency to levitate, and St. Teresa of Avila and St. Ignatius of Loyola often returned from states of trance with knowledge of another level of reality. Clairvoyant and precognitive experiences as well as healings were common among the desert fathers in Egypt, and among many others. To canonize a saint, in fact, the Catholic Church requires proof of miraculous events attributed to the saint, usually healings. In the recent past, this is not fully demanded.

There are some 12,000 canonized saints in the Catholic Church and more than a 1000 are in the run for canonization. Even today, the Catholic Church requires two miraculous phenomena as attestation of the saintly life of the canonized. We may question whether it is necessary to connect miraculous phenomena to a saintly life. Some of the phenomena associated with saints whose lives we are familiar with are the following:

1.  Visions: By visions we mean the perception of an object or a place that is naturally invisible to human beings.

2.  Revelations: These are manifestations of hidden truths that are not normally accessible to human beings. Many of the devotions like the devotion to the Sacred Heart, Rosary etc. came into widespread practice because their power was revealed to certain people.

3.  Reading of thoughts: The knowledge of the secret thoughts of others or of their internal state without prior communication is possible for some saints.

4. Stigmata: These phenomena are the spontaneous appearance of wounds resembling Christ's wounds. St. Francis of Assisi and Padre Peo are well known for their stigmata.

5. Bilocation: This phenomenon is the simultaneous presence of a physical body in two distinct places at the same time, the well attested example is that of St. Philip Neri.

6. Tele-transportation: The instantaneous movement of a material body from one place to another without passing through the intervening space is called tele transportation.

7. Levitation: The elevation of the human body above the ground without visible cause and its suspension in the air without natural support is called levitation. Plenty of such instances have been recorded in other religions also.

8. Bodily incombustibility: This is the ability of human body to withstand the natural laws of combustibility.

9. Inedia: This is the absolute and total abstinence from all nourishment beyond the limits of nature.

10. Mystical Aureoles and Illuminations: This is characterized by emanation of light from the body of an individual especially during ecstasy and contemplation.

11. Sweet odours: It has been noted that sweet odours were emanated from the living or the dead body of certain people. They were classified as miraculous by Pope Benedict XII.

12. Blood prodigies, Bodily incorruptibility and absence of rigor mortis: These phenomena are well attested in the lives of saints. In India, St. Francis Xavier can be cited as an example.

## 1.  Cult of the Saints

In the Catholic Church, a saint is anyone in Heaven, whether recognized on earth or not. The title, "Saint" denotes a person who has been formally canonized, that is, officially and authoritatively declared a saint by the Church. There are many persons that the Church believes to be in Heaven who have not been formally canonized and who are otherwise titled "saints," because of the fame of their holiness.

In the year 993 A.D, Pope John XV canonized for the first time Bishop Ulrich of Augsburg on 31 January, on the petition of the German ruler. Before that time, the popular "cults," or venerations of saints had been local and spontaneous. Pope John XVIII subsequently permitted a cult of five Polish martyrs. Pope Benedict VIII later declared the Armenian hermit Symeon a saint, but it was not until the pontificate of Pope Innocent III that the Popes reserved to themselves the exclusive authority to canonize saints. Once a person has been canonized, the deceased body of the saint is considered holy as a relic. The remains of saints are called holy relics and are usually used in churches. Saints' personal belongings may also be used as relics. Formal canonization is a lengthy process, often of many years or even centuries. If the application is approved, the candidate may be granted the title, "Venerable." Further investigation may lead to the candidate's beatification with the title "Blessed." Then a minimum of two important miracles are required as proofs from God through the intercession of the candidate for formal canonization as a saint. Finally, after all these procedures are complete, the Pope may canonize the candidate as a saint for veneration by the universal Church.

Identified in its origins with the cult of martyrs, devotion to the saints first took the form of praise and imitation but by the 3rd century, the efficacy of intercession of the saints was clearly recognized. The 4th and 5th centuries saw the extension of cult from martyrs in the strictest sense to those whose ascetic life could be considered equivalent to martyrdom. By 4OO A.D, saints were being invoked for needs. Though the early theologians carefully distinguished between veneration of saints and adoration of God, there were at first no suitable terms to express the distinction. The Middle Ages produced in the West a flowering of popular devotions to the saints with pilgrimages, increasing veneration of relics, extensive naming of patrons and feasts developing into civic festival. The council of Trent,[5] appealing to apostolic tradition and to the teaching of the Fathers and Councils, directed that the faithful should be instructed that the saints intercede for them and that it is good and useful to invoke them to obtain benefits from God through Christ, the sole Redeemer.

## 2. Veneration of Relics

A **relic** usually consists of the physical remains of a saint or the personal effects of a saint or a venerated person, preserved for the purposes of veneration as a tangible memorial. One of the earliest sources that show the efficacy of relics is found in 2 Kings 13: 20–21. Elisha had died and was buried. Moabite raiders used to enter the country every spring. Once, while some Israelites were burying a man, suddenly they saw a band of raiders; so, they threw the man's body into Elisha's tomb. When the body touched Elisha's bones, the man came to life and stood up on his feet.

The Second Council of Nicaea in 787 drew on the teaching of St. John Damascene, that homage or respect is not really paid to an inanimate object, but to the holy person, and indeed, the veneration of a holy person itself is honour paid to God.

The Council decreed that every altar should contain a relic, making it clear that it was already the norm, and it remains the norm to the present day in the Catholic and Orthodox churches. The veneration of the relics of the saints reflects a belief that the saints in heaven intercede for those on earth. A number of cures and miracles have been attributed to relics, not because of their own power, but because of the holiness of the saint they represent.

Many tales of miracles and other marvels were attributed to relics beginning in the early centuries of the church. They became popular during the Middle Ages. The tales were collected in books of hagiography such as the *Golden Legend* or the works of Caesarius of Heisterbach. These miracle tales made relics much sought-after during the Middle Ages. By the late Middle Ages the collection of, and dealing in, relics had reached enormous proportions, and had spread from the church to royalty, and then to the nobility and merchant classes.

Relics were used to cure the sick, to seek intercession for relief from famine or plague, to take solemn oaths, and to exert pressure on warring factions to make peace in the presence of the sacred. Courts held relics since Merovingian times. An active market developed for relics. Relics entered commerce along the same trade routes followed by other portable commodities. Canterbury was a popular destination for English pilgrims, who travelled to witness the miracle-working relics of Thomas Becket, the sainted archbishop of Canterbury who was assassinated by knights of King Henry II in 1170. After Becket's death, his successor and the Canterbury chapter quickly used his relics to promote the cult of the as-yet-uncanonized martyr.

As holy relics attracted pilgrims and these religious tourists needed to be housed, fed, and provided with souvenirs, relics became a source of income not only for the people of the pilgrim centres that held them, but for the abbeys, churches, and towns en route. Relics were prized as they were portable. They could be possessed, inventoried, bequeathed, stolen, counterfeited, and smuggled. They could add value to an established site or confer significance on a new location. Offerings made at a site of pilgrimage were an important source of revenue for the community who received them on behalf of the saint.

## 3.   Pilgrimages

The veneration of holy places is the oldest expression of popular piety. The journey of the empress mother Helena to the Holy Land around A.D. 300 inaugurated the cult of the relics through the alleged discovery of the holy cross. The cult of martyrs and saints led to the establishment of shrines outside Palestine, which later were developed into Pilgrim places. The idea that the martyrs are present at the places of martyrdom (e.g., Peter's tomb at Vatican) secured a prominent position for holy places connected with the cult of saints and martyrs. The cult of martyrs was developed especially in the Roman catacombs. Preachers might warn that pilgrimages did not necessarily bring one nearer to God and that one must not worship the martyr, but at the popular level such exhortations seemed useless. Today pilgrimages to Lourdes, Fatima, Velengani etc. are a part of religious piety. The miracles that happen in these places are well attested despite the strict scientific investigation in many cases.

## 4.    Charisms and Healing

The notion that prayer, divine intervention or the ministrations of an individual healer can cure illness has been popular throughout history. Miraculous recoveries have been attributed to a myriad of techniques commonly lumped together as "faith healing."

In 1 Cor12, St. Paul gives two types of extraordinary gifs. They are major extraordinary gifts and minor extraordinary gifts. Healing comes under minor extraordinary gifts or Charisms. This is based primarily on Jesus' healing actions in the Gospel and on two Scripture texts: these signs will follow believers; "they will ...........lay their hands on the sick who will recover[6]"; and "if anyone of you is ill, he should send for the elders of the Church. They must anoint him with oil in the Name of the Lord and pray over him and the prayer of faith will save the sick man."[7]

We must grant that healing is a special, social, charismatic gift; that Christ healed many people; that he gave his immediate disciples this power and ordered them to use it. They did use it and healing was part of the ordinary ministry of the disciples. Right through the centuries this power has been exercised, though sparingly, by the saints. It seems to have been revived considerably during the Charismatic Renewal.

Technology has led to phenomenal advances in medicine and has given us the ability to decrease the morbidity and improve the outcome. The notion that prayer, divine intervention or the ministrations of an individual healer can cure illness has been popular throughout history. Miraculous recoveries have been attributed to a myriad of techniques, commonly lumped together as 'faith healing,' and it is attributed to spiritual means.

Believers assert that healing of a person can be brought about by religious faith through prayers and/or rituals that stimulate a divine presence and power toward correcting disease and disability.

In 1910, Sir William Osler, Regius Professor of Medicine at Oxford University, published a now classic paper in the *British Medical Journal* entitled, "The Faith that Heals."[8] In his article, Osler extolled the many virtues of faith, especially in relation to healing, and medicine. Sixty-five years later, Dr Jerome D. Frank, pre-eminent Johns Hopkins psychiatrist, revisited these themes in a seminal paper also named, "The Faith that Heals."[9]. Frank concurred with Osler that faith "is an important topic that is conspicuously absent from the medical school curriculum and explained that the concept has significant connotations for healing besides its obvious religious context. For Frank, the most powerful single stimulator of the patient's expectant faith is, of course, the physician himself. Osler had something important in mind that he articulated clearly: that the impact of faith is very real and cannot be denied, as honest clinical observation will attest. At the beginning of the last decade, one comprehensive overview found over 1,200 empirical studies of religion and health that had been published in the peer-reviewed literature.[10] According to these various reviews, between three quarters and in excess of 90% of these studies obtained positive findings, depending upon the health outcome in question. The implication of this research and writing, taken together, seems clear: faith can heal. Expressions of faith are potentially therapeutic. So, how does faith heal? One possibility is by *suggestion*. Another possibility is something akin to *hypnosis*—an altered state of consciousness induced by faith or a faith healer that enables one to marshal what today we might refer to as self-soothing psychophysiological mechanisms that enhance coping and mitigate pain, symptoms, and morbidity. Yet another possibility is the salutary *emotional effect* of faith— as a result of affirming God's omnipotence, omniscience, omnipresence, beneficence, and the possibility of a personal relationship through which contact and communion with God is possible. Other hypothetical mechanisms or mediators of a faith-healing connection are related to the idea of a *flow of energy* as in Reiki.

If prayers do heal, and they surely do, at least a part of their effect must be placebo: the belief that they will heal. To say that the part of healing brought about by the act of praying could come through the placebo effect, is not to say it is fake, but rather to give it a very real explanation. However, the placebo effect is brought into action, whether by making a prayer or by believing in a pill, once in play, it acts through well-defined nerve pathways and molecules—molecules that can have profound effects on how immune cells function. A part of prayer's effect might come from removing stress—reversing the effect that a burst of hormones that can suppress immune function. Scholarly work on these "well-defined nerve pathways and molecules" and their effects on immune function is a key to making sense of placebos, and, that is perhaps how faith heals. Psychoneuroimmunology, the study of the interactions between behaviour, brain, and immunity, may lead us to identify mechanisms of action that underlie the workings of the various psychological theories and constructs identified above. Discoveries of the past three decades have led us to recognize that the central nervous system is intimately connected to the immune system. The brain regulates immunity, and this immune modulation constitutes both neurological and psychological functions. The latter, in turn, may encompass the activity of behaviours and thoughts and emotions.

## 5.    Possession and Exorcism

The word Exorcism comes from the Greek word 'exorkismos,' which means binding by oath or making a demand. It is the religious or spiritual practice of purportedly evicting demons from a person or an area they are believed to have possessed. In the Catholic Church exorcism is performed in the name Jesus. The word 'exorcism' is not mentioned in the Bible, but from the ministry of Jesus it is very clear that he used exorcism. He healed the sick and cured the people who were possessed. Unlike other Jewish exorcists, Jesus never used secondary means in his exorcisms, such as fumigations, rings, roots or herbs. He commanded the demons with authority and they obeyed his command. When the disciples were unable to drive out a demon, Jesus explains that there are different types of demons, and some of these can only come out by prayer.[11] Catholic Church affirms that the power of exorcism which Jesus exercised at one time is handed over to the disciples.[12] And having called his 12 disciples together, he gave them power over unclean spirits, to cast them out and to heal all kinds of diseases and every sickness.[13]

Performing exorcism was central to the ministry of Jesus, which is mentioned in all the four gospels. Often the word "driving out" or "casting out"[14] is used for the expulsion of demons. The term "possessed" as denoting possession by a demonic presence, is mentioned a total of seventeen times in the gospels, though it is alluded in the Old Testament as well.[15] Following the examples and directives of Christ, the Church has always believed in and fought against the power of Satan in this world by baptizing the faithful, administering the sacraments, dying for faith (martyrs), and doing charitable works (corporal and spiritual works of mercy). Christians were deeply influenced by what they had learned of their master's dealing with evil spirits, and there was on their part frequent use of the charismatic gifts of healing the sick and driving out devils. But the prayers and forms used for exorcism in the first centuries have not come down to us, outside the ones used in baptism.[16] Exorcism became part of the baptismal rite somewhere around 200 A.D.

The fifteenth century marks the existence of exorcism practiced by both Catholic priest and the lay person. It is believed that every Christian has power to cast out demons; therefore, laypeople also exercised exorcism to drive out demons in the name of Jesus Christ. These exorcists used the Benedictine formula "Step back, Satan" around this time. In the late 1960s, Roman Catholics rarely performed exorcism but by 1970s, popular films like 'The Exorcist' and literature revived interest in the ritual, with thousands claiming to be possessed by the demon. In 2014, a Roman Catholic organization called 'International Association of Exorcists,' received approval of the Vatican.

According to Canon law (1172), "No one can legitimately perform exorcisms over the possessed, unless he has obtained special permission from local Bishop." The Canon goes on to point out: "Such permission from ordinary is to be granted only to a priest endowed with piety, knowledge, holiness, prudence, integrity of life.". Therefore, only priest with proper experience, holiness and knowledge of theology should undertake to perform exorcism. In the Catholic Church, a Bishop or a priest, appointed by him, can perform exorcism. By the virtue of priesthood, all priests can perform exorcisms of water, oil, salt, incense, etc. It is not a solemn exorcism. Every priest performs exorcism while administering the sacrament of baptism, but it is a minor exorcism.

## Signs of Genuine Demonic Possession

The Encyclopaedia of Catholic Doctrine defines demonic possession as[17], "the tangible proof of the existence of the devil and a visible manifestation of his power" within a person. According to the Roman Rite of Exorcism, there are often particular signs that accompany one who is possessed by demons.

- An ability to speak with some facility in a strange tongue or to understand it, when spoken by another.

- The faculty of divulging future and hidden events.

- The display of powers which are beyond the subject's age and natural condition.

The Roman Ritual defines the phenomena of demonic possession in the following way: "Apart from the general power over men that providence allows to the tempter, there is also a special and terrible satanic influence. It is called possession, the domination by the demon over man's bodily organs and his lower spiritual faculties; or in the later times, a distinction is made between possession and obsession, the latter connoting a lesser grade of demonic disturbance[18]." It goes to note that possession can mean that Satan has gained mastery over the will of the person.

When someone approaches a priest for exorcism, the following signs may indicate that there is possession:

a.  Medicine is ineffective

b.  Hatred towards Holy Eucharist, Crucifix, Sacraments, blessings etc.

c.  History of the Occult, Satanism and Addictions in the life of the person coming for exorcism.

## Types of Diabolic Activity

i.  Infestation: This is the first stage where begins the demonic activity in one's life. There are some signs and symptoms which include (but are not limited to) things happening around them such as objects being moved, severe and repeated temptation seeing shadow figures and sensing offensive odours that are not naturally caused, and inciting of fear, anxiety, worry and panic.

ii. Diabolic Obsession: This occurs when the Evil One focuses much of his attack on an individual. Through this type of attack, he may not gain full control or possession over the person. Obsession may manifest itself and extraordinary in strong temptation to commit grave, mortal sin. Spiritual Oppression, though to some degree different, is sometimes associated with obsession as well. Many of the saints have experienced this form of attack, including St. Padre Pio, St. John Vianney and St. Gemma Galgani having incurred no personal sin on their part.

iii. Possession: Full Diabolic possession occurs when the Devil invades a person's body and exerts full control over the faculties of the individual, "manipulating them as one would a puppet." The power of the Devil, however, is restricted only to the body, as he cannot invade or take control of the soul, intellect, or will of the person. One can likewise be in the state of grace spiritually, and yet still encounter diabolic possession, not having been responsible of the imprudent behaviour which may have contributed to the possession itself

a. **Voluntary Possession:** This is a form of diabolic possession that is *intentional* on the part of the person who is possessed. The most serious and dangerous form of demonization is when one has integrated with a demon and has further deteriorated to a level of being totally possessed, and literally sought it.

b. **Involuntary Possession:** Involuntary possession means that the person afflicted was not overtly asking for the Devil or a demon to possess him or her. This is one of the most difficult categories for people to grasp and come to terms with.

## Guidelines for Exorcism

The following guidelines or rules according to the Roman Rite of Exorcism should be kept in mind while doing an exorcism.

1. First, the exorcist must be sure that he is dealing with a possessed person, not someone with psychological problems.

2. To do this, he must distinguish possession from superstition. Sometimes people believe they have been affected by the evil eye or some other form of black magic. They should not be denied spiritual aid, but no exorcism should be carried out in such case.

3. The following are the signs of possession: a sudden capacity to speak unknown languages, abnormal physical strength, the disclosure of hidden occurrences or events, and a

vehement aversion to God, the Virgin Mary or the Saints, sacramental rites and religious images, especially the cross.

4.  In difficult cases, while always respecting the secrecy of the confessional, the exorcist may consult spiritual guides or church-recommended physicians or psychiatrists before deciding to perform an exorcism.

5.  In the case of Non-Catholic Christians and unusual situations, the exorcist priest can leave the final decision to his diocesan bishop, who may consult outside experts.

6.   Exorcism should, if possible, be carried out with the consent of the possessed person, and with the awareness of the person's individual physical and mental condition.

7.   Exorcism should always be performed as an expression of Catholic faith and should never give the impression that it is a superstitious or magical event.

8.  At the same time, an exorcism should never turn into a "show" for the faithful. For that reason, media representatives and journalists must not be allowed to attend. The success or failure of an exorcism is not to be announced or published.

9.  Relatives and friends may assist at an exorcism, if exorcist deems it helpful, since they are able to help with their prayers. The possessed person should pray to God, particularly before the ritual, and strengthen his soul by receiving the sacraments of Baptism, Confession and Communion.

## 6.    Haunted Places and Blessings

A haunted house/mansion/castle is a house, or a building often perceived as being inhabited by disembodied spirits of the deceased who may have been former residents or were familiar with the property. Parapsychologists attribute haunting to the spirits of the dead and the effect of violent or tragic events in the building's past such as murder, accidental death, or suicide. Explanations that are more scientifically attributed, mentioned for a haunted house, include misinterpreting noises naturally present in structures, waking dreams, suggestibility, and the effect of toxic substances in environments that can cause hallucinations.

The first step is to determine whether or not there is a legitimate case of haunting. Not all hauntings are alike, and some may exhibit a variety of phenomena. Some hauntings feature a single phenomenon - such as a particular door slamming shut that occurs repeatedly - while others consist of many different phenomena, ranging from odd noises to full-blown apparitions. Only after exhausting all explanations of natural forces, should one suspect an experience to have haunted element in it.

Given below is a partial list of phenomena that might indicate a house is haunted:

- **Unexplained Noises:** Footsteps, knocks, banging, rapping, scratching sounds, sounds of something being dropped. Sometimes these noises can be subtle and other times they can be quite loud.

- **Doors, Cabinets, Cupboards Opening and Closing** - Most often, these incidents are not seen directly. The one who experiences either hears the distinct sounds of the doors opening and closing or the one who experiences will return to a room to find a door open or closed when they are certain that it was left in the opposite position.

- **Lights Turning off and on** - Likewise, these events are seldom seen occurring, but the lights are switched on or off when the person living in the house knows they were not left that way. This can also happen with TVs, radios and other electrically powered items.

- **Items Disappearing and Reappearing** - these phenomena – 'the DOP Effect' (Disappearing Object Phenomenon), is sometimes common but ignored or neglected. Objects which are normally placed in one place somehow disappear and later appear in the same place – as an example 'A set of car keys' – which a person has placed in a spot- disappears. Sometime later, the keys are found exactly in the place the person placed them. It is as if the object was borrowed by someone for a short time, and then returned. Sometimes they are not returned for days or even weeks, but when they are, it is in an obvious place that could not have been missed by even a casual search.

- **Strange Animal Behavior** - a dog or a cat or other pet behaves strangely. Dogs may bark at something unseen. Cats may seem to be "watching" something across a room. Animals have sharper senses than humans do, and many researchers think their psychic abilities might be more finely tuned also.

- **Unexplained Shadows** - the sighting of fleeting shapes and shadows, usually seen out of the corner of the eye - many times, the shadows have vaguely human forms, while other times they are less distinguishable or smaller.

- **Feelings of being Watched** - this is not an uncommon feeling and can be attributed to many things, but it could have a paranormal source, if the feeling consistently occurs in a part of the house at a time.

- **Feelings of being Touched** - the feeling of being watched is one thing, and feeling like you are being touched is quite another. Some people feel something brush past them, something touching their hair or "a hand" on the shoulder. Some feel a gentle poke, push or nudge.

- **Cries and Whispers** - on occasion, muffled voices, whispering and crying can be heard. Sometimes it is music from some unknown source. People hear their names being said. This phenomenon, as is true for the one above, gains more credibility, if more than one person hears or sees the same thing at the same time.

- **Cold or Hot Spots** - cold spots are classic haunting symptoms, but any instance of a noticeable variance in temperature without a discernable cause could be evidence.

- **Unexplained Smells** - the distinct fragrance of a perfume that one does not have in one's house - this phenomenon comes and goes without any apparent cause and may accompany other phenomena, such as shadows, voices or psychokinetic phenomena. Foul odours can happen in the same way.

- **Moving or Levitating Objects** - dinner plates sliding across the table; pictures flying off walls; doors slamming shut with great force; furniture sliding across the floor.

- **Physical Assault** - scratches, slaps and hard shoves. This kind of personal assault is extremely rare, but obviously highly disturbing.

- **Apparitions** - physical manifestation of a spirit or entity. These phenomena are also very rare and can take many forms: human-shaped mists or forming mists of some indistinguishable shape; transparent human forms that disappear quickly; and most rarely, human forms that look as real and solid as any living person, but disappear even while being viewed.

## 7.   Blessings / Sacramentals

There are seven sacraments in the Catholic Church, which according to Catholic theology were instituted by Jesus and entrusted to the Church. Sacraments are visible rites seen as signs and efficacious channels of the grace of God to all those who receive them with the proper disposition. But, sacramentals are sacred signs which bear a resemblance to the sacraments. They signify effects, particularly of a spiritual nature, which are obtained through the intercession of the Church. By them men are disposed to receive the chief effect of the sacraments, and various occasions in life are rendered holy.[19]

Blessings are not sacraments; they are sacramentals and, as such, they are held to produce the following specific effects:

- Excitation of pious emotions and affections of the heart and, by means of these, remission of venial sin and of the temporal punishment due to it.

- Freedom from power of evil spirits.

- Preservation and restoration of bodily health.

- Various other benefits, temporal or spiritual.

Not all these effects are necessarily inherent in any one blessing; some are caused by one formula and others by another, nor are they infallibly produced. It depends altogether on the Church's suffrages that persons using the things blessed derive supernatural advantages. There is no reason to limit the miraculous interference of God to the early ages of the Church's history, and the Church never accepts these wonderful occurrences unless the evidence in support of their authenticity is unimpeachable.

For the blessing of the structures, objects, houses, things and so on, sacramentals like Holy water, Oil and salt are used.

The Catholic Church holds that things used in daily life, particularly in the service of religion, should be rescued from evil influences and endowed with potency for good. The principal liturgical blessings recognized and sanctioned by Church are contained in the Roman Ritual. The Ritual has blessings for houses and schools and for the laying of their foundation stones for stables and every other building of any description for which no special formula is at hand.

Holy Water: Holy water is the water blessed by a priest with solemn prayer, to beg God's blessings on those who use it, and protection from the powers of darkness. Recent research in water shows that it may hold memories. Through the 1990's, Dr. Masaru Emoto performed a series of experiments observing the physical effect of words, prayers, music and environment on the crystalline structure of water.[20] Emoto hired photographers to take pictures of water after being exposed to the different variables and subsequently frozen so that they would form crystalline structures. The results were nothing short of remarkable. It is astounding that the words and thoughts that come out of us have this effect on water crystals.

Holy Oil: The spiritual meaning of oil is deep and rich. Through the centuries, oil has provided food, medicines, heat and light for man. Holy oil is used in the blessings of the persons and things. Specifically, for anointing of the seriously sick and critically injured, and for the possessed as well.

Salt: Since salt cannot corrupt and even keeps things from corruption, salt is a sign of everlasting life. Recalling the blessed salt scattered over the water by the prophet Elisha and invoking the protective powers of salt and water, Salt is used to drive away the power of evil. Salt may also be blessed for use as a sacramental, using the same prayer as is used during the preparation of holy water. This salt may be sprinkled in a room, or across a threshold, or in other places as an invocation of divine protection. The belief is that this salt will keep demons and possessed persons away from a home and crossing a line made of salt.

## 8.     Witchcraft and Witch Hunt

In witchcraft, there is involved the idea of a diabolical pact or at least an appeal to the intervention of the spirits of evil. In such cases this supernatural aid is usually invoked either to cause the death of some person, or to awaken the passion of love in those who are the objects of desire, or to call up the dead, or to bring calamity or impotence upon enemies, rivals, and fancied oppressors.

Under the Roman Empire in the third century, the punishment of burning alive was enacted by the State against witches who caused another person's death through their enchantments.[21] The ecclesiastical legislation followed a similar but milder course.

The Council of Elvira in 306 A.D refused the holy Viaticum to those who had killed a man by a spell (*Canon 6*) and adds the reason that such a crime could not be affected "without idolatry," which probably means, without the aid of the Devil. Similarly, canon 24 of the Council of Ancyra in 314 AD, imposes five years of penance upon those who consult magicians, and here again the offence is treated as being a practical participation in paganism. This legislation represented the mind of the Church for many centuries.

Altogether, it may be said that in the first thirteen hundred years of the Christian era we find no trace of that fierce denunciation and persecution of supposed witches which characterized the cruel witch hunts of a later age. In the earlier centuries a few individual prosecutions for witchcraft took place, and at some of them, torture as permitted by the Roman civil law, apparently took place.

On the other hand, after the middle of the thirteenth century, the then constituted Papal Inquisition began to concern itself with charges of witchcraft. Alexander IV, indeed, ruled in 1258 that the inquisitors should limit their intervention to those cases in which there was some clear presumption of heresy. It was at any rate at Toulouse in 1275, we have the earliest example of a witch burned to death after judicial sentence of an inquisitor.

The Bull, "Summis desiderantes affectibus," was issued by Pope Innocent VIII in 1484. Its direct purpose was simply to ratify the powers already conferred upon Henry Institoris and James Sprenger as inquisitors, to deal with persons of every class and with every form of crime, and it called upon the Bishop of Strasburg to lend the inquisitors all possible support.

Around the year 1485, the book "Malleus Maleficarum" (the hammer of witches) was published. This work is divided into three parts, the first two of which deal with the reality of witchcraft as established by the Bible, as well as its nature and horrors and the manner of dealing with it, while the third lays down practical rules for procedure, whether the trial is conducted in an ecclesiastical or a secular court. There can be no doubt that the book, owing to its reproduction by the printing press, exercised great influence on witch hunts. It contained, indeed, nothing that was new.

The penal code known as the Carolina in1532 decreed that sorcery throughout the German empire should be treated as a criminal offence, and if it purported to inflict injury upon any person, the witch was to be burnt at the stake. In 1572, Augustus of Saxony imposed the penalty of burning for witchcraft of every kind, including simple fortune-telling.

There were witch trials in all countries including the Americas. Perhaps the most effective protest on the side of humanity and enlightenment was offered by the Jesuit Friedrich von Spee, who in 1631, published his "Cautio criminalis," and fought against the craze by every means in his power. At the end of the seventeenth century, the persecution almost everywhere began to slacken, and early in the eighteenth, it practically ceased.

## 9.    Devotion to Angels

Although angels belong to the world we cannot see, they have been known by civilizations and cultures for thousands of years. Theologians debate their nature; psychologists analyze them; philosophers' probe into the rationale for their existence; musicians and lyricists emulate their celestial harmony; artists depict them in varied shapes and forms; persons of faith testify to experiencing the presence of angels. Ultimately, the existence of angels, like the existence of God, can be acknowledged only in faith. Angel is derived from the Greek word 'angelos' which means "messenger'; the Hebrew word is ma'ak, which also means 'messenger,' and it is used to describe any agent God sends to do his will.

A sixth-century Syrian monk, called Dionysius, viewed all of creation as being bonded in successive stages from the lowliest creature on earth to the highest in heaven. In "the celestial hierarchy," he arranged the angels into nine choirs in a gradual ascent to God's heavenly throne. His listing of angels' choirs, adopted by Thomas Aquinas, is still recognized in Christian angelology.[22]

Worship and praise are one of the tasks which God has entrusted with angels. This is the main activity portrayed in heaven.[23] One of the major tasks, which angels do for God is that of being his messengers. They serve as messengers to communicate God's will to people. They helped reveal the law to Moses,[24] and served as the carriers of much of the material in Daniel, Revelation and the Gospels. Sometimes angels work as guides. They gave instructions to Joseph about the birth of Jesus,[25] to the women at the tomb, to Philip,[26] and to Cornelius.[27] Angels do the job of a provider. God has used angels to provide for the physical needs to many people such as food for Hagar,[28] Elijah[29] and Christ after His temptation.[30] Angels protect people out of physical danger, as in the cases of Daniel and the lions and his three friends in the fiery furnace.[31] Many times, angels work as delivering agents of God and getting God's people out of danger once they are in it. Angels released the apostles from prison in Acts

5 and repeated the process for St. Peter in Acts 12. Angels do the strengthening and encouraging role for God's people in their struggles. Angels strengthened Jesus after His temptation, encouraged the apostles to keep preaching after releasing them from prison[32] and told St. Paul that everyone on his ship would survive the impending shipwreck.[33] God often uses angels as His means of answering the prayers of His people.[34] They were used by God to punish sinners such as to David for his vanity in taking a census of the great number of his people, and to kill the firstborns of the Egyptians.

The cult of the Angels is found expressed very early in Christian tradition, in the writings of the Fathers. With St. Benedict in the West begins a tradition of faith, love and devotion to Holy Angels that grew steadily from Pope Saint Gregory the Great to Saint Bernard, the chief and most eloquent exponent of the cult and devotion to the Guardian Angels. The names of the holy Angels were always regarded as a powerful invocation in time of need and distress.

The church celebrates the feast of the Archangels, St. Michael, Saint Gabriel and Saint Raphael.

## 10.  Novenas

The word novena comes from the Latin "novem" meaning nine. It is a nine days' private or public devotion in the Catholic Church to obtain special graces. Though they are not part of liturgy, it remains a "popular devotion." Therefore, novena is an act of pious Roman Catholic devotion, consisting of private or public prayers for nine successive days in belief of obtaining special intercessory graces.

A novena is a vocal prayer, or series of vocal prayers that you commit to praying over an extended period. These prayers are usually linked to a specific devotion or liturgical celebration. They are also very often linked to a specific intention that we are praying for – we can offer a novena to petition God for a special grace, like the healing of a sick person or the conversion of someone who is far away from God. The words of the novena will reflect all these factors. They will remind us of the meaning of the liturgical celebration, the virtues of a saint, or the goodness of God. And the combination of prayers will usually give you a place to insert your personal petition. It is important to remember, however, that novenas are not magic formulas. They are prayers. They are means through which we can enter conversation with God. The recitation of novena prayers is primarily found in the Roman Catholic Church, while some members of the Anglican, Eastern Orthodox and Lutheran Churches also share in an effort for church renewal. The prayers are often derived from devotional prayer books, or they consist of the recitation of the rosary or of short prayers.

The nine-day period of prayer has its origin in the Book of Acts. After Jesus' Ascension into heaven, the Apostles, the Blessed Virgin, and some of Christ's other followers all "joined in continuous prayer"[35] for nine days, until the dramatic coming of the Holy Spirit on Pentecost.

There are four main classified types of novenas:

1. Novenas of mourning: such as the novena made during the novemdiales - the nine-day period following the death of a Pope.

2. Novenas of preparation, or "anticipation," such as the Christmas or Easter Novenas.

3. Novenas of prayer (to different saints).

4. The indulgenced novenas.

In general, we pray novenas for the same reason that we pray at all: God deserves our praise, and we need his grace. Novenas are prayers and all the benefits that prayer always brings are also brought by novenas. This form of prayer, however, has some special characteristics.

First, they provide a channel for strong spiritual sentiments or desires. Sometimes, our hearts are so full of sorrow, anxiety, hope, or thirst for holiness, that it is hard for us to find the words to express ourselves. In a crisis, a novena can channel our apprehension in a positive way: entrusting our deeply felt needs to God through the intercession of a saint, for example. Novenas put clear parameters around deep spiritual sentiments, enabling us to have confidence that we are keeping them in harmony with God and his will.

## 11. Stigmata

Etymologically the word Stigmata comes from the Greek word *stizo*, which means "to prick." Stigmata refers to the five wounds that were inflicted on Jesus' body during his crucifixion, and to similar wounds resembling Jesus' puncture marks that have mysteriously appeared on others. Stigmata are traditionally located at the specific spots where Jesus' flesh is said to have been pierced during his crucifixion: namely his wrists (two wounds from nails), his shins (one wound from a nail), his head (bleeding from a crown of thorns), and his heart (one wound inflicted by a Roman soldier's spear). A person who spontaneously bears one or more of these wounds is called a "stigmatic."[36] There are instances of stigmatics who have portrayed wounds that are not corresponding to the five wounds of Christ or any other wounds Jesus got during his crucifixion. The famous example of such stigmata is the special case of Fr. Zlatko Sudac who depicts a cross like mark on his forehead.[37]

The causes of stigmata are largely mysterious, but some observers suggest that stigmata are found in deeply pious individuals who overwhelmingly empathize with the suffering of Jesus. Reactions to this phenomenon are varied, ranging from doubt and scepticism to praise and reverence.

There are no known cases of stigmata for the first 1,200 years after Jesus died. The first person said to suffer from stigmata was St. Francis of Assisi (1182-1226), and after that there have been a few hundred cases and most of them are women. Famous among them are St Catherin of Sienna, St Theresa of Avila, Ann Catherin Emeric etc and the most recent ones such as Padre Pio, Elizabeth Sanches, Audri Moris Sanches, Olivia Catri Revas, Jullia Kim, Jorgia Bongervani.[38]

St. Francis of Assisi is the first recorded stigmatic in Christian history. The following is the account of Brother Leo, one of the saint's companions on the mountain, how St. Francis of Assisi got his stigmata. In 1224, two years before his death, he embarked on a journey to Mt. La Verna for a forty day fast.[39] One night near the feast of the Exaltation of the Cross, Francis was kneeling outside his hut. Dawn was near. It was bitingly cold, and the stars were shining brightly in the sky. Suddenly there was a dazzling light. It was as though the heavens were exploding and splashing forth all their glory in millions of waterfalls of colours and stars. And in the centre of that bright whirlpool was a core of blinding light that flashed down from the depths of the sky with terrifying speed until suddenly it stopped, above a pointed rock in front of Francis. It was a fiery figure with wings, nailed to a cross of fire. Two flaming wings rose straight upward, two others opened out horizontally, and two more covered the figure. And the wounds in the hands and feet and heart were blazing rays of blood. The sparkling features of the Being wore an expression of supernatural beauty and grief. It was the face of Jesus, and Jesus spoke. Then suddenly streams of fire and blood shot from His wounds and pierced the hands and feet of Francis with nails and his heart with the stab of a lance. As Francis uttered a mighty shout of joy and pain, the fiery image impressed itself into his body, as into a mirrored reflection of itself, with all its love, its beauty, and its grief. And it vanished within him. Another cry pierced the air. Then, with nails and wounds through his body, and with his soul and spirit aflame, Francis sank down, unconscious, in his blood. This is how it is believed that the event might have taken place.[40] The scientists have a very different explanation regarding the stigmata and this vision of St Francis of Assisi. First, they consider this vision a hallucination as a result of his ill health.

Many stigmata wounds show recurring bleeding that stops and then starts, and at times after receiving Holy Communion. A large percentage of stigmatics have shown a high desire to receive Holy Communion frequently and are seen living with minimal (or no) food or water for long periods of time, except for the Holy Eucharist, and some exhibit loss of weight. Famous example of this is Padre Pio, himself. It is said that he carried out fasting for twenty-one days on no other nourishment but the sacred host.[41]

A stigmatic's wounds do not appear to clot but stay fresh and uninfected. And the blood from the wounds is said, in some cases, to have a pleasant, perfumed odour, known as the Odour of Sanctity. A stigmatic (i.e. the person suffering from stigmata) may have one, several, or all of these wound marks. Moreover, they may be visible or invisible, and they may be permanent, periodic, or temporary in appearance. Some sceptics would attribute such wound marks on a person to some pathology or even to a psychological condition without considering any notion of the supernatural. Of course, the Church too strives first to ascertain that the origin is not of natural cause and look for supernatural evidence to prove that the stigmata is truly a sign from God. Moreover, the Church would also like to ensure that the stigmata is not a sign from Satan to cause some spiritual frenzy and lead people astray. Accordingly, since the stigmata is a sign of union with our crucified Lord, the genuine stigmatic must have lived a life of heroic virtue, have endured physical and moral suffering, and have almost always achieved the level of ecstatic union with him in prayer.

The Catholic Church has wrestled with the authenticity of stigmata from its inception, investigating whether they are seeking money or some tangible connection to God. Many stigmatics have been caught red-handed, faking their wounds. In fact, out of all the dramatic accounts of stigmatics through the centuries, only one has been officially sanctioned by the Church, the first one, that of St. Francis of Assisi. The Church is very careful to officially declare someone genuinely partaking in Christ's passion through stigmata and will never publically accept or officially declare someone stigmatic, if not necessary. The reason behind is that it is difficult to explain this phenomenon and to prove its authenticity, but it really is easy to fake it.

There are millions of paintings of Jesus' crucifixion, but no one knows for certain how exactly Jesus was crucified and where his wounds should be. Did they crucify him by driving the nails through his palms or his wrist, is another question that interests the scientists. Works of art, countless writings, and every cross in the churches in Christendom suggests that nails were directly driven through his palms and the arches of his feet.[42] But a bizarre experiment in the early 20th century by French surgeon Pea Barbe proved that the palms could not support the weight of the body and came to the conclusion that Jesus must have been nailed through his wrist.[43] No sooner had this discovery made known to the stigmatics around the world, the wounds began to migrate from the palms to the wrists. A famous example of such a stigmatic is Fr. James Bruse. But the modern technology helped Doctor Zugabi to put Barbe's findings to the test, and he concluded that the person who is crucified to the cross through his palms can support the body of his weight, and that the nails do not tear up the palms, because the weight is redirected to the cross through the legs, helping the palm not to tear apart. He pointed out the fact that Barbe did not account for the legs being pinned to the cross; he estimated the weight and the consequence of free hanging.[44] This discovery made the wrist bleeders look hoax and the palm bleeders, the true and genuine ones, but one thing is for sure, that our beliefs and thinking play a significant part in the phenomenon of stigmata.

## 12.  Private Visions and Prophecies

Many Saints and Blesseds have claimed private revelations from God of various kinds throughout the history of the Church. Some of them have been accepted by the Church. For example, the following apparitions and their messages were accepted as genuine:

- Sacred Heart of Jesus apparitions to Saint Margaret Mary Alacoque.

- Sacred Heart of Jesus apparitions to Blessed Mary of the Divine Heart Droste zu Vischering.

- Revelation of the Divine Mercy to Saint Faustina Kowalska.

- Revelation of the Scapular of the Sacred Heart to Estelle Faguete.

Therefore, it must be true that God gives private revelation to some persons. There are nine apparitions of the Virgin Mary, each a type of private revelation that has gained approval from the leadership of the Church. Examples of the apparitions include Our Lady of Guadalupe, Fatima, Lourdes, La Salette, and others.

On the other hand, there have been several claims of private revelations, including claims of apparitions of the Virgin Mary that have been rejected by the faithful and condemned by the Church.

The prophetic element, despite the end of public revelation, retains unique importance in the Church. Consequently, it is important how we can distinguish authentic visions, heavenly messages, prophecies etc. from human and diabolical ones.

According to the teachings of the Church, public revelation has come to an end with the death of the Apostles. All the subsequent revelations are private, and they do not belong to the deposit of faith. But private revelation continues in the life of the individual. The church must deal with them only to ascertain whether they are consistent with the deposit of faith.[45] Devotions like the Rosary, the devotion to the Sacred

Heart of Jesus etc. thrived in the Church because of private revelations.

In principle, the Holy Spirit can act upon the Church through any one of its members to announce what the Spirit requires of it. This is the essence of post-apostolic, prophetic private revelations. God is inspiring a member of the church with his imperative in a concrete historical situation. How such a private revelation passes from the individual to the church, or to the greater part of it, whether by actual preaching or by the influence of example or otherwise, is a secondary matter.

In private revelations, one cannot exclude the possibility of self-induced hallucinations or the fact of God's using visionary phenomena as the vehicle for a genuine revelation. Given then the possibility of divine revelations through visions, how do such religious experiences come about? We know that they must come from God in some sense, but the precise meaning of their divine origin is not always clear. For example, although it is theoretically possible in a private vision for God to act upon a human person, since the vision also involves activity on the part of the visionary himself, it seems likely that his personal psychological structure will also enter the very constitution of the vision. As a result, the line dividing the natural from the supernatural in such experiences is often quite obscure.

Visions are time and space bound and related to the present. In a broad sense, history of Christianity would be unthinkable without the prophetic and visionary element. Karl Rahner opines that if such phenomena were present in Old Testament, it is also possible today. In Christ, God's final and definitive revelation has taken place: all revelations, since then, have a different theological character. In apostolic period, this gift was received by the possession of the Spirit and this is a permanent gift of the Church.

So, to see the authenticity of Private Revelations, one must see whether they belong to the deposit of faith. "It is then impressed upon that the *public revelation* ceased with the death of the apostles, with the result that subsequent revelation does not belong to the church's deposit of faith, being simply 'private revelations,' that hence, there can be no duty to believe them with "Catholic faith." And the Church can and must deal with such private revelations only so far as she must ascertain whether they are consistent with the deposit of faith, and consequently whether the Catholics may believe in them."[46]

In 2012, the Vatican published some norms for recognizing authentic private revelations.[47]

The newly published guidelines set out a three-stage process by which a legitimate church authority can come to a decision regarding claims of apparitions or revelations.

First, the claim should be initially judged, "according to positive and negative criteria." This investigation can include an assessment of the "personal qualities" of any alleged seers as to their "psychological equilibrium, honesty and rectitude of moral life, sincerity and habitual docility towards ecclesiastical authority, the capacity to return to a normal regimen of a life of faith, etc."

Any potentially authentic revelation must also be of "true theological and spiritual doctrine and immune from error," and should be producing a "healthy devotion and abundant and constant spiritual fruit" such as a "spirit of prayer, conversion, testimonies of charity, etc."

Second, if the local church authorities come to a favourable initial conclusion, they can permit some form of public devotion, while continuing "overseeing this with great prudence."

. Third, a final judgment can then be passed "in light of time passed and of experience" with special regard to "the fecundity of spiritual fruit generated from this new devotion."

Ecclesiastical approval "essentially means that its message contains nothing contrary to faith and morals."

There are well known mysterious prophecies like that of Nostradamus about the prophecies of the centuries, Alois Irlmaier's prophecies, the third secret of Fatima given by Sr.Lucia, Saint Malachy's prophecies on the popes, etc. Nostradamus' prophecies are so mysterious and open for multiple interpretations that one can never be sure what they mean. Normally after an event, people say this was what he meant. These prophecies have nothing to do with faith.

# Conclusion
## Supernatural as the Foundation of the Church

Supernatural phenomenon permeates the very fabric of Christianity. The Christian faith abounds in spiritual beings, visions, healings, miracles of all kinds, and the culminating experience of Christ's appearance after his death. The entire theme of the after-life is central to the life of the Church. Christ presented us with a vision of the unseen world from which he emerged after death to demonstrate a higher revelation of the after-life beyond the simple fact of mere immortality.

Being born into a supernatural structure, the Christian is in communion with the rest of the Church. There is a communion and communication in this psychic structure. The process of growth within this structure is achieved through the sacraments and the sacramentals. While helping individuals to experience the Christian reality, it also keeps them in touch with the world. Communication and relationship is established through prayer. If one prays, one expects an answer, and then there is belief in communication with another world.

## Endnotes

[1] 1 Cor. 12:28

[2] 1 Cor. 13:1

[3] Lk. 12:31

[4] Kerr John, The Mystery of Magic and the Occult, SCM Press, Great Britain, 1972

[5] Council of Trent, session 25 Dec 1563

[6] Mk. 16; 18

[7] (Jam. 5:14, 15)

[8] Osler W. The faith that heals. *Brit Med J.* June 18 1910:1470-1472

[9] Frank JD. The faith that heals. *Johns Hopkins Med J.* 1975; 137:127-131

[10] Koenig HG, McCullough ME, Larson DB. *Handbook of Religionand Health.* New York, NY: Oxford University Press; 2001

[11] Mark 9:14-29 ; Matt 17:14-21 ; Luke 9:37-43

[12] CCC, 1115

[13] Mt.10:1

[14] Mt.7:22; 8:16; 8:31; 9:34; 10:8; 12:24; 12:27-28; Mk 1:32, 34, 39; 3:15; 3: 22; 6:16; 9:38; 16:9; Lk 4:41; 8:2; 8:27, 30, 33, 35, 38; 10:17; 11:15, 18-20; 13:32

[15] Micah 2:11

[16] Roman Ritual1953

[17] The Encyclopedia of Catholic Doctrine, 1912, p.172-173

[18] Roman Ritual, p.162

[19] Catechism of the Catholic Church, 1667

[20] http://highexistence.com/water-experiment/

[21] Julius Paulus, "Sent.", V, 23, 17

[22] Altemose, C. (2006). *What You Should Know About Angels.* Mumbai: St Paul Publications

[23] Isa. 6:1-3; Rev 4-5

[24] Acts 7:52-53

[25] Mt. 1-2

[26] Acts 8:26

[27] Acts 10:1-8

[28] Gen. 21:17-20

[29] 1 Kings 19:6

[30] Mt. 4:11

[31] Daniel 3, 6

[32] Acts 5:19-20

[33] Acts 27:23-25

[34] Daniel 9:20-24; 10:10-12; Acts 12:1-17

[35] Acts 1:14

[36] "Stigmata- A Definition," *Super Natural Phenomena,* http://www.newworldencyclopedia.org/entry/Stigmata (accessed January 28, 2016)

[37] "Stigmata," *Interview with FR. Zlatko Sudac,* http://www.stjeromecroatian.org/eng/frsudac.htm (accessed January 28, 2016)

[38] *Is Stigmata Real -A National Geographic Television and Film Production,* Directed by Chad Cohen, 2005

[39] "Stigmata," *Christianity and Saints,* http://www.catholic.org/saints/stigmata/ (accessed January 28, 2016)

[40] "Blood gender and power," *Religion and Truth,* http://www2.kenyon.edu/Depts/ Religion/ Projects/ Reln91/ Blood / Christianity/stigmata.htm (accessed January 28, 2016)

[41] Rev. Charles Mortimer Carty, *Padre Pio The Stigmatist,* London (Radio Replies Press St. Paul, Minnesota, U.S.A, 1955), 15

[42] "Blood gender and power," *Religion and Truth,* http://www2.kenyon.edu/Depts/ Religion/ Projects/ Reln91/ Blood / Christianity/stigmata.htm (accessed January 28, 2016)

[43] *Is Stigmata Real -A National Geographic Television and Film Production,* Directed by Chad Cohen, 2005

[44] Ibid

[45] Rahner Karl *Visions and prophecies*, Herder and Herder, New York, 1963, p.19 – 20

[46] Rahner Karl *Visions and prophecies*, p.19–20

[47] https://www.catholicnewsagency.com/news/vatican-publishes-guidelines-on-apparitions-private-revelations

# Chapter 5

# Popular Occult Beliefs and Practices

The aim of this chapter is to give an account of the occult practices being practised or performed by the general public. Some of these are practised as entertainment or for fun. Some may engage in them just for fun. Some of these practices can invite unintended harm to the individual. So, this chapter introduces the reader to the background of these practices and their implications.

## 1. Mediums and Channelling

Mediumship or channelling is about those who are still here in the physical world connecting with those who have died. It can also be about connecting two living human beings, channelling information from one to the other.

The Bible has a story about a medium who communicated with the dead. King Saul demanded the witch of Endor to put him in touch with the dead prophet Samuel.[1] It was Samuel who had anointed him as King earlier. This medium was apparently renowned among the domain of mediums. The person whom she contacted was no fake Samuel because the text treat has treated him as the real Samuel. But this Samuel was not at all happy about being contacted. He truthfully issued God's final doom on Saul and his sons, specifically because Saul was not following God's command. The next day, Saul found out first-hand about being in the realm of the dead.

Why are people seeking spirit communication, through a medium? Spirit communication helps bring together that which seems to have become separated and lost through death. They hope to re-establish interaction with their loved ones. They seek spirit communication because they want to know whether their loved ones are alive in another world. Mediumship is supposed to answer this kind of concerns.

Mediums can be differentiated into three different types, depending on what they claim to experience. The first include the physical mediums, which can receive verbal messages from the dead and produce physical disturbances during the sessions. The physical disturbances can be levitation, object movement, and knocking or rapping.

The second category of mediums is the mental mediums. These mediums speak with the dead mainly by going into a trance and becoming 'possessed' by the dead person's spirit and a control entity. In some cases, when a spirit is channelled, the medium's height, figure, voice, and even body marks like moles or tattoos appear to be like the spirit's, regardless of its gender.

The third category of mediums is the psychic mediums. They do not go into a trance but remain fully conscious during their communications with the spirits.

Some of the phenomena and experiences alleged to be associated with mental mediums include:

• Receiving information from the deceased that can be verified.

- Ability to 'read' the past and the present of a client.

- Object movement, disappearance and reappearance.

- Apparitions.

- Various physical manifestations.

- Examples and instances of ESP.

- Levitation.

- Unexplained lights.

- Hearing music.

- Being physically touched.

- Physical manifestations of hands, feet, heads, etc.

- Automatic writing.

It is difficult to verify the truth behind what the medium claims. Sometimes, many of their claims may be fake. They may have great abilities to read people and so what they say may be based on that. I am not denying that some people may have the ability to sense vibrations around people and interpret them.

## 2.    Dowsing and Water Divining

Many people believe that a successful site for a well can be chosen by a gifted person walking over the land with a 'divining rod'. Although tools and methods vary widely, most dowsers probably still use the traditional forked stick, which may come from a variety of trees. Other dowsers may use keys, wire rods, pendulums, various kinds of elaborate boxes or electrical instruments.

In the classic method of using a forked stick, one fork is held in each hand with the palms upward. The bottom or the butt end of the "Y" is pointed skyward at an angle of about 45 degrees. The dowser then walks back and forth over the area to be tested. When she/he passes over a source of water, the butt end of the stick is supposed to rotate or be attracted pointing downward.

There have been many contradictory theories about the agent behind water divining, and there is still no general consensus. Many dowsers claim that they respond to earth "rays" or magnetism. Some believe that a kind of clairvoyant faculty is involved. It is possible that several factors are involved, varying with the talent and skill of the diviner.

Some water exists under the Earth's surface almost everywhere. This explains why many dowsers appear to be successful. To locate groundwater accurately, however, as to depth, quantity, and quality, a number of techniques must be used. Hydrologic, geologic, and geophysical knowledge is needed to determine the depths and extent of the different water-bearing strata and the quantity and quality of water found in each.

Some people seem to be able to locate buried pipes with the aid of rods or twigs. One theory is that the muscles in the body react to some electromagnetic effect caused by the presence of the metal or the water flowing through the pipe; the rods then amplify this effect so that the searcher becomes aware of them. Another theory is that some diviners know from their experience and local knowledge where groundwater is likely to be located which subconsciously causes the reaction.

The technique of using a pendulum to acquire information not only about an object's location but also of its character has become known as radiesthesia. Antelope and wild pigs have curved horns and tusks which are similar in shape to the traditional forked twig and both these species are very successful in finding hidden water sources. Could it be that their built-in dowsing rods help in some way? The best human dowsers can work with their bare hands, so it is possible that even animals without antennas can navigate in this way. The roots of trees are positively geotropic – they grow directly towards the source of gravity – but they also seek out sources of water – they do dowsing.

Apparently, some people are more sensitive to the presence of water as in the case of wild animals.

## 3.    Use of Ouija Board

As a method of supposed communication with the spirit world, the Ouija board has terrified countless fun-loving children and served as a plot vehicle in a number of Hollywood films. Ouija boards have their roots in Spiritualism, which began in the United States in the late 1840s. The new movement was led by mediums, who claimed to be intermediaries between the living and the dead. As a part of the spiritualist movement, mediums began to employ various means for communication with the dead. Following the American Civil War in the United States, mediums did significant business in presumably allowing survivors to contact lost relatives.

There were a number of ways mediums made followers believe that they were communicating messages from those who had died. One such effort was the new talking board which was developed in Ohio in 1886. It was 18 by 20 inches and featured the alphabet, numbers, and the words 'yes,' 'no', 'good evening', and 'goodnight'; the only other necessary object was a planchette – a little table three or four inches high, with four legs that can be moved. Operating the board was made easy. Two people sit around the board and each grasp the planchette with the thumb and forefinger at each corner. Then the question is asked, 'Are there any communications?' Pretty soon one person thinks that the other person is pushing the table. The other person does the same. And the planchette moves around to 'yes' or 'no.' Then they go on asking questions and the answers are spelled out by the legs on the table resting on the letters one after the other.

These types of talking boards became very popular, and in 1890 Elijah Bond, Charles Kennard and William H.A. Maupin had the idea to turn the board into a toy. They filed the first patent for a game they called the Ouija board, which looked and operated much like the talking boards into a toy. The patent was granted in 1891. The name, according to Kennard, was an ancient Egyptian word meaning "good luck." Others say that the word Ouija comes from amalgamation of the French 'oui' for 'yes,' and German 'Ja' for 'yes.'

Scientific explanation for the source of messages generated was that it is a result of the ideomotor effect. This psychological phenomenon was first described in 1852 by William Benjamin Carpenter who, theorized that muscular movement can be independent of conscious desires.[2] The ideomotor effect occurs when someone moves an object without being conscious of their actions. This combined with a strong subconscious need for an answer, like what one might feel when using an Ouija board, leads to players moving the planchette without any knowledge of doing so.

No matter how innocent Ouija boards may seem, playing with Ouija boards can be an opening for dangerous experiences to invade our hearts and minds.

## 4. Poltergeist Phenomena

Poltergeist cases are characterized by a series of apparently anomalous physical phenomena such as the sudden movement of objects without any apparent force acting upon them, and rapping or knocking sounds that do not seem to have any clear source. Like cases of ghosts and apparitions, these occurrences have a long tradition steeped in myth, folklore, and superstition.

In folklore and parapsychology, a poltergeist (German for "pounding ghost") is a type of ghost or other supernatural being supposedly responsible for physical disturbances such as loud noises and objects being moved or destroyed. Most accounts of poltergeists describe movement or levitation of objects such as furniture and cutlery, or noises such as knocking on doors. Poltergeists have traditionally been described as troublesome spirits who haunt a particular person instead of a specific location. Such alleged poltergeist manifestations have been reported in many cultures and countries.

Here's a list of the most common signs of poltergeist phenomena:

- Electrical disturbances or electrical objects working on their own: it is reported that when some people enter a room, the overhead light and lamps flicker. In the presence of some other people, the electrical gadgets switch on by themselves or switch off.

- Rapping or banging on walls or other unexplained noises: in some places, you can hear footsteps, and when you look, there is no one there. Sometimes, you can hear rapping or knocks without anyone being present.

- Objects moving or being thrown around by themselves: in the presence of some people, objects move. Objects may fall from shelves on their own or move from one place to another place. The movement of physical objects like this can be quite dramatic.

- Disappearing Objects Phenomena (DOP): DOP involves an object that a person had just been using or that he invariably keeps in one place. When the person wants to use the object, it is gone. The person looks high and low for the object, often getting others involved in the search, but it cannot be found. A short time later, or perhaps the next day, the person is surprised to find the object returned to the spot where it is always kept or in some other obvious place where the search should have found it. When examining such occurrences as DOP, we must first consider the most ordinary possibility: that the person simply misplaced the object or forgot where he/she had put it. This, in fact, probably accounts for most reported DOPs.

- Strange or unusual smells: in some cases, suddenly the overpowering scent or fragrance fills the room. All kinds of smells can enter your house from the outside, even from a passing car, so such scents might not necessarily mean poltergeist.

- Physical attacks: some people have reported being physically attacked. They see scratches and experience pain. Some get physically slapped and there is no one to be seen. Very often these experiences are reported from cemeteries and haunted places.

It is generally accepted that poltergeist phenomena is not caused by good or evil spirits, but rather psychic manifestations of stress or anxiety, often associated with the presence of a teenager. In other words, when exploring a paranormal explanation, poltergeist activity is often attributed to psychokinesis, or the ability to affect physical objects with one's mind.

Other possible natural explanations may include:

- moving air currents.
- vibrations caused by underground water currents.
- electromagnetic disturbances.
- seismic activity.
- infrasound.

Many of the common mis-perceptions regarding the poltergeist phenomenon began in 1982, when Steven Spielberg and Tobe Hooper released their frightening special effects movie called *Poltergeist*. The movie was a hit at the box office and has since come to be seen as a classic horror movie.

Poltergeist activity centers on people and is often associated with the presence of adolescent children, leading many to suspect that childhood attention-seeking pranks are involved.

Indeed, many poltergeist reports were proven to have been faked by children and teenagers. Since poltergeist activity is a psychic effect rather than a spirit-based one, the investigator should try to determine who the agent is - the person who is generating the telekinetic activity. Various kinds of stresses can be the cause of this activity, including emotional, physical, psychological, and even hormonal stresses. So the investigator should try to examine the personal and family dynamics and may very well need to seek the help of a counselor.

## 5.   Automatic Writing

A person writing something without his/her voluntary and psychic involvement and awareness is called Automatic writing. And there are people who claim that they have experienced automatic writing. Some of them are Fernando Pessoa, George Hyde-Lees, the wife of William Butler Yeats, Helene Smith, poet Robert Desnoscand etc. Fernando Pessoa said that he felt he was owned by something else and sometimes he felt a sensation in the right arm which he claimed was lifted into the air without his will.[3] Joan Baez, American Singer/Songwriter, who experienced automatic writing, says "It seems to me that those that have been any good, I have nothing much to do with the writing of them. The words have just crawled down my sleeve and come out on the page.[4] All automatic writers unanimously claimed that they were unaware of what they were writing and for whom they were writing. Automatic writing can happen in a trance or waking state.[5] Altered states of consciousness seems to be a condition for automatic writing.

## 6.   Tarot Cards

The Oxford Dictionary defines 'Tarot' as a set of playing cards first used in Italy in the 14th century, and later on used in fortune telling.[6] From the late 18th century until the present time the tarot has also found use by occultists for divination.[7] For some, Tarot is a tool for unlocking the subconscious mind and bringing thoughts and feelings into conscious awareness.[8]

Playing cards first entered Europe in the late 14th century, probably from Egypt, with suits of Swords, Batons or Polo sticks, Cups, and Coins. These suits were very similar to modern tarot divination decks and are still used in Spanish and Portuguese playing card decks. It is important to note that there is no one universal standard deck for Tarot Card interpretations.

The reader spreads the cards and chooses and appropriate ones, based on the client's inquiries, so that the client can get as much 'food for thought' as possible from the meanings and interpretations. The images on the cards may be woven together in a cohesive story for the client, linking the meanings with the inquiry and also bringing up key themes in the life journey of the client.[9] It's important to note, however, that tarot does not answer questions in a yes/ no format. That is why many would refrain from calling such an occult practice as fortune- telling. A tarot session suggests various guidelines and raises questions for the seeker to contemplate, especially if there's a choice involved or a paradigm shift that is needed.

## 7.   Astrology

Astrology is one of the ancient sciences in the world. Centuries of studies, observations, experiences and expressions are included in this subject. Various civilizations have developed and contributed their valuable knowledge to this science. The central principle of astrology is integration within the cosmos. The individual, the Earth and its environment are viewed as a single organism, all parts of which are correlated with each other. Cycles of change that are observed in the heavens are, therefore, reflective of similar cycles of change observed on earth and within the individual.[10] Astrology has failed to produce answers to the questions of modern science and lacks in objectivity and consistency. But today many still believe in astrology and there are very many who pursue this study to become astrologers.

The first definite reference to astrology in Rome comes from the orator Cato, who in 160 B.C warned farm overseers against consulting with Chaldeans, who were described as Babylonian 'star-gazers.' During the Renaissance, court astrologers would complement their use of horoscopes with astronomical observations and discoveries. Many individuals now credited with having overturned the old astrological order, such as *Tycho Brahe, Galileo Galilei* and *Johannes Kepler,* were themselves practicing astrologers. Astrologers were theorists, researchers, and social engineers, as well as providers of individual advice to everyone from monarchs downwards.[11] Among other things, astrologers could advise on the best time to take a journey or harvest a crop, diagnose and prescribe medicines for physical or mental illnesses, and predict natural disasters. This underpinned a system in which everything—people, the world, the universe— was understood to be interconnected, and astrology co-existed happily with religion, magic and science.[12] At the end of the Renaissance the confidence placed in astrology diminished, with the breakdown of Aristotelian Physics and rejection of the distinction between the celestial and  sublunary realms, which had historically acted as the foundation of astrological theory.[13]

The zodiac is the belt or band of constellations through which the Sun, Moon, and planets move on their journey across the sky. Astrologers noted these constellations and so attached a significance to them. Over time they developed the system of the twelve signs of the zodiac, based on the twelve of the constellations through which the sun passes in a year. In modern Western astrology the signs of the zodiac are believed to represent twelve basic personality types or characteristic modes of expression. Western astrology is based mainly upon the construction of a horoscope, which is a map or a *chart* of the heavens at a particular moment. The moment chosen is the beginning of the existence of the subject of the horoscope, as it is believed that the subject will carry with it the pattern of the heavens from that moment throughout its life. The most common form of horoscope is the natal chart based on the moment of a person›s birth; though in theory, a horoscope can be drawn up for the beginning of anything, from a business enterprise to the foundation of a nation or state.[14]

Today astrology is a part of day to day life of many people. Some might take it seriously, but others take it out of curiosity or in jest. Newspapers often print astrology columns which purport to provide guidance on what might occur in a day/ week in relation to the sign of the zodiac that included the sun when the person was born. These predictions are vague or general so much so that even practising astrologers consider them of little or no value. Experiments have shown that when people are shown a newspaper horoscope for their own sign along with a newspaper horoscope for a different sign, they judge them to be equally accurate on the average. Other tests have been performed on complete, personalized horoscopes cast by professional astrologers, and have shown similarly disappointing results, contrary to the claims of professional astrologers.

## 8.    Palmistry

Each person carries an exclusive pattern of lines in his/her hands. The dermis of the skin has a distinctive assortment of loops, whorls, and arches in the finger tips and on the palm. Every hand seems to have its own idiosyncrasies and the palmists insist that this mean something. Many genetic disorders can be detected on the palm or on the nails.

There are an enormous number of nerves ending in the hand in sensors of heat and cold, pressure and pain. So many of these make direct connections with the brain. The brain, the nervous system, and the sense organs are all derived from the ectoderm of the embryo at the same time as the skin. Their common origin means that they maintain very close connections throughout life, and it is not at all unreasonable to assume that many internal events will show up externally through the skin. So, theoretically, there is a no reason why it should not be possible to make judgments about a person's prevailing mental condition, and therefore, about his personality from signs appearing on the skin. The connection between internal physical and mental states and the crease lines of the palm is more difficult to establish. No consistent theory, which is applicable to all, has been found. More than the lines, clairvoyance and self-fulfilling theories, may account for the truth of the predictions.

## 9.    Conscious Control of Involuntary Body Functions

The conscious control of involuntary functions is common place in yoga, Zen and some African cults. Pulse rate, breathing, digestion, sexual function, metabolism, and kidney activity can all be influenced by and at will. Skilled practitioners, after years spent perfecting what amounts to a system of conditioned reflexes, can slow the heartbeat almost to the vanishing point, reduce the body temperature to what would normally be lethal levels, and reduce their respiration to no more than one breath every few minutes. In this state the whole organism is reduced to a condition like that of a hibernating animal and can be buried alive for days without ill effects. The reflexes that normally make us shy away from intense pain can be diverted so that nails are driven through the limbs and spikes through the cheeks or tongue. And while this is being done, the sympathetic nervous system can be locally suppressed or stimulated so that bleeding is prevented or encouraged. The pupils which normally respond to light and emotion can similarly be controlled. There is nothing supernatural about any of these abilities; many of them have been objectively studied and imitated in the laboratory. It takes time and practice to cultivate the right paths of control. Some of these skills are developed purely as a means of livelihood by some people, but in many instances, they are simply by-products of the process of self-realization.

## 10.  Black Mass

A Black Mass is a parody of the Catholic mass sometimes practiced by wealthy opponents of the Church in the Dark Ages.[15] Modern Satanists sometimes perform a 'black mass' for theatrical effect, but it is not a standard practice in Satanism or in modern witchcraft.

As early Christianity was becoming stronger and growing in influence, the early Church fathers described a few heretical groups practicing their own versions; some of them were of sexual nature, used violence and created scandals. Beginning with the Latin writings of the *Goliards*, the Roman Catholic

Mass was drawn from or elaborated upon to create parodies of it for certain Church festivities in the Middle Ages. Consequently, there was a Mass parody called "The *Feast of Asses,*" in which *Balaam's Ass* (from the Old Testament) would begin talking and saying parts of the Mass. A similar parody was the *Feast of Fools.*[16] Other Middle Age parodies of the Mass, also written in *ecclesiastical Latin,* which were known as *"drinkers' Masses"* and "gamblers' Masses," which lamented the situation of drunk, gambling monks, and instead of calling to God, called to *"Bacchus"* (the God of Wine). The Catholic Church, however, eventually reacted by condemning them as sacrilegious and blasphemous.

Furthermore, the Rite of the mass was not completely fixed. There was a place at the end of the offertory, when the priest could insert private prayers for various personal needs of the people. These types of personal prayers within the Mass spread the institution of the low mass. People would hire the priests to perform various masses for their own needs such as blessing of crops or cattle, achieving success in some enterprise, obtaining love, or cursing enemies which was done by inserting the enemy's name in a 'Mass for the dead,' accompanied by burying an image of the enemy. However, such practices were condemned.

In the early 20th century H.T.F Rohdes' popular book, *The Satanic Mass*, published in London in1954, was a major inspiration for modern versions of the Black Mass. Rhodes claimed that, at the time of his writing, there did not exist a single first-hand source which actually described the rites and sermonized on the nature of a Black Mass. In the year 1968 and 1969, there appeared the first two books about satanic rituals, both entitled as the Satanic Mass.

While the Black Mass is erroneously associated with witches and witchcraft, it does play a distinct part in witchcraft history and the history of the humankind. The Black Mass was more of a ceremony that attracted the wealthier and educated dissenters of the Church. There is no set Black Mass ritual; rather the ceremony is a parody on the holy Catholic Mass. This ceremony includes the inverting of the cross, spitting and stepping on the cross, stabbing the host and other obscenities. The magical significance of the Black Mass rests in the belief that the Holy Mass involves the miracle of the transubstantiation, that is, the mystical changing of the bread and wine into the body and blood of Jesus Christ. If the priest can affect this miracle within the Holy Mass, then it is reasoned that someone could affect similar magic in other masses for harmful purposes such as cursing a person to death, etc. According to the erroneous understanding of some of these people, the easiest way to achieve this is to use an already consecrated host. In some places, there was a craze to buy consecrated host for these purposes. So, the Catholic Church has taken more secure ways of distributing communion.

## 11.   Out of Body Experiences (OBE)

Out of body experience can be expressed as an experience in which the centre of awareness to the person occupies temporarily a position which is spatially remote from his or her body. People experiencing OBE find themselves instantaneously exteriorized in the immediate vicinity of the physical body, looking down on the environment and perceiving it in an apparently realistic fashion. OBE is also called astral travel and some people have claimed of astral flights to far-off lands.

In an OBE, people seem to be awake and feel that their 'self' or centre of experience is located outside of the physical body. They report seeing their body and the world from an elevated extracorporeal location. The subject's reported perceptions are organized in such a way as to be consistent with this elevated visuo-spatial perspective.

The administration of different pharmacological substances has presumably been used since immemorial times in ritual practices to induce abnormal experiences including OBEs. They include marijuana, opium, heroin, mescaline, ketamine, and LSD. OBEs in association with general anaesthesia have also been reported.

## 12. Near Death Experiences (NDE)

A near-death experience is a personal experience associated with death or impending death. Such experiences may encompass a variety of sensations, including detachment from the body, feelings of levitation, total serenity, security, warmth, the experience of absolute dissolution, and the presence of a light. Near-Death Experiences have accompanied and fascinated humanity since times immemorial and have long been associated with the occult. Many authors have even argued that these experiences provide evidence for mind-brain independence or even the persistence of life after death. The neurology of NDEs have been studied by neurologists and cognitive scientists, as they have investigated the functional and neural mechanisms of bodily awareness and self-consciousness in specific brain regions. Although many different theories have been proposed about the supposed underlying brain processes, neurologists and cognitive neuroscientists have paid little attention to these experiences. In different life-threatening situations, people can sometimes experience vivid illusions and hallucinations as well as strong mystical and feelings often grouped under the term of near-death experiences. These medical situations seem to involve cardiac arrest, perioperative or post-partum complications, septic or anaphylactic shock, electrocution, coma resulting from traumatic brain damage, intracerebral hemorrhage or cerebral infarction, hypo glycaemia, asphyxia, and apnoea. Systematic studies on the incidence of NDEs in verified medical conditions only exist for patients with cardiac arrest.

The phenomenological elements of NDE as reported by Moody[17] are:

a.  an overwhelming feeling of peace and well-being, including freedom from pain.

b.  the impression of being located outside one's physical body.

c.  floating or drifting through darkness, sometimes described as a tunnel.

d.  becoming aware of a golden light.

e.  encountering and perhaps communicating with a 'presence' described by Moody as a 'being of light.'

f.  having a rapid succession of visual images of one's past.

g.  experiencing another world of much beauty, perhaps meeting the spirits of deceased relatives and acquaintances with whom one also might communicate.

These experiences would offer strong support for the survival hypothesis, if it could be shown to be what it superficially seems to be a literal separation of the soul from the body and its passage to some paradisial realm of post-mortem existence. However, Neuroanatomical models suggest that damage to the bilateral occipital cortex may lead to visual features of NDEs such as seeing a tunnel or lights, and "damage to unilateral or bilateral temporal lobe structures such as the hippocampus and amygdala" may lead to emotional experiences, memory flashbacks or a life review.[18]

## 13. Apparitional Experiences

Tales of ghosts and other apparitions have been reported in all cultures. Something that unexpectedly appears or becomes visible, apparently not by natural means is called an apparition. An apparition is someone you see or think you see but who is not really there as a physical being. Apparition The supernatural appearance of a discarnate, immaterial, bodiless, ethereal figure otherwise known as a ghost or spirit (the soul or essence) of a person left after the earthly, physical form has ceased. Apparitions may be either a ghost or spirit.

Nearly 20% U.S. adults says they have seen or been in the presence of a ghost, according to a 2009 Pew Research Centre survey.[19] An even greater share, a 29% says that they have felt in touch with someone who has already died. However, actual apparitions are very rare. Some people experience visual phenomena such as quick flashes of light, odd wisps of smoke or dark shadows. Some others experience strange sounds, footsteps, ghostly whispering and knocking. Some others speak of odd odours of flowers, cigars, feeling cold shiver, doors opening on their own accord, clocks running fast or slow. It looks like most of the apparitions are hallucinations.

## 14. Reiki and Pranic Healing

These are two methods which claim to heal people.

Reiki is a Japanese technique, administered by "laying on hands," and is based on the idea that an unseen "life force energy" flows through us, and is what causes us to be alive. If one's "life force energy" is low, then we are more likely to get sick or feel stress, and if it is high, we are more capable of being happy and healthy. The word 'Reiki' is made of two Japanese words, 'Rei' which means "God's Wisdom or the Higher Power" and 'Ki' which is "life force energy." So Reiki is actually "spiritually guided life force energy." However, there is no scientific evidence to support claims that the so-called vital energy actually exists, nor is there conclusive evidence that Reiki is useful for any health-related purpose. But despite the fact that Reiki has not been proven effective at treating certain health conditions, Reiki is not a harmful practice either.

Pranic healing is a claimed energy-healing system, founded and promoted by Choa Kok Sui (1952–2007), a Filipino entrepreneur and philanthropist. The healing modality claims that 'prana' can heal ailments in the body by contributing to the person's energy field.

The fundamental principles of Pranic Healing are

- Principle of Self- Recovery – The innate ability of every living being to heal itself.

- Principle of Life Force – Healing process can be accelerated by increasing the 'pranic' life force of the individual.

Pranic Healing is supposed to correct imbalances in the body's energy field and transfers life force to the patient. This life force can also be characterized as universal energy; it is not the healer's energy. Trained Pranic Healers access and transmit universal energy to the patient, using specific frequencies and techniques for specific diseases and conditions. Pranic Healing is done without touching. It is a three-step process that substantially accelerates the body's innate ability to heal at all levels: physical, emotional, mental and spiritual.

- Checking - Scanning for energy abnormalities.

- Cleansing - Removing energy abnormalities: cleansing is used to remove dirty or diseased energy in the body and to eradicate blockages in the energy channels.

- Replenishing and revitalizing with life force,- Energizing: the transference of fresh 'prana' or life energy to the body. Once it is applied, the cleansing process is completed.

The efficacy of Reiki and Pranic healing seems to produce more of a placebo effect.

## 15. Synchronicity

The experience of meaningful coincidences is universal. They are reported by people of every culture, every belief system, and every time period. *Synchronicity* examines the evidence for the human influence on the meaningfulness of events, and the way the modern computational model of the mind predicts how we create meaning. Synchronicities are those moments of "meaningful coincidence," when the boundary dissolves between the inner and the outer. Synchronicity was one of Carl Jung's most profound, yet least understood discoveries, in part because it cannot be appreciated until we personally step into and experience the synchronistic realm for ourselves. Because it is so radically discontinuous with our conventional notions of the nature of reality, the experience of synchronicity is so literally mind-blowing that Jung contemplated this phenomenon for over twenty years before he published his thinking about it. Jung's synchronistic universe was a new world view which embraced linear causality while simultaneously transcending it. The synchronistic universe is beginning-less in that we are participating in its creation right now, which is why Jung calls it "an act of creation in time."[20]

To illustrate what he meant by the word synchronicity, Jung brings up an experience he shared with a patient of his. This particular patient was very caught up in her head, and the analysis was seemingly going nowhere. She was stuck, trapped in the self-created prison of her own mind. Jung realized there was nothing he could do. She had an impressive dream the night before, in which someone offered her a golden scarab – a valuable piece of jewelry. At the moment she was telling Jung the dream, there was tapping on the office window. Jung opened up the window and a scarabaeid beetle, whose gold-green color closely resembles that of a golden scarab, flew into the room. Jung caught the beetle in his hand, handed it to her and said "Here is your scarab."

The shock of recognition in the synchronistic moment, in which Jung's patient realized her dream of the previous night was being both literally and symbolically enacted in her waking life, pierced through her resistance and cracked her defensive shell wide open. At the moment of synchronistic transmission, a fundamental shift in perception took place within her which inwardly transformed her and made her receptive in a new way. From that point on, Jung commented, "The treatment could now be continued with satisfactory results."

There was no conventional, linear causal link between the patient's dream and the beetle tapping on the window the next day. But there was clearly a correspondence and meaningful connection between the two co-related events which was not based on linear causality. In addition, the patient did not cause or create the synchronicity, which was acausal and happened of its own accord. And yet, in some mysterious way, the beetle tapping on the window was intimately related to her.

## 16.  Numerology

Pythagoras, the great Greek mathematician and mystic, proclaimed that the world is built upon the magical power of numbers. According to his doctrines, numbers contained within them the essence of all that is in the natural and the spiritual worlds. According to numerologists, each number possesses a certain power that exists in the occult connection between the relations of things and the principles in nature which they express. All that humans are capable of experiencing can be reduced to the digits, one to nine. These single numbers are derived from the simplification of all combinations of numbers to their basic essence. This essence then vibrates through the single digit. There are so many different systems of numerology that to give a definition which would include all of them is not an easy matter. The belief in numerology originated from the belief that spoken word has power.

Numerology had not found favor with the Christian authority and was assigned to the field of unapproved beliefs along with astrology and other forms of divination and magic. However, despite the Church's resistance to numerology, there have been arguments made for the presence of numerology in the Bible and religious architecture. For example, the numbers 3 and 7 hold strong spiritual meaning in the Bible. The most obvious example would be the creation of the world in 7 days. Skeptics argue that numbers have no occult significance, and cannot by themselves influence a person's life. Skeptics, therefore, regard numerology as a superstition.

Contemporary numerologists use their various systems to produce assessments of an individual's personality traits, behavior patterns, and to predict compatibility and a possible course of future events for their clients. Depending upon the numerological system, the first and most important number derives from a person's date of birth and it is determined by reducing the numbers of that date into single digits. However, there can be no proof for the efficacy of numerology.

## 17. Crystal Gazing

It is an established fact that certain sensitive persons are affected by the presence of water, and they become water dowsers. Similarly, some others may be similarly affected by the presence of basaltic rocks beneath the surface of the land. Coming into a locality they may describe things which have already taken place, as if they were presently conscious of them, or as if the events were taking place before their eyes. At other times, they may describe events which are subsequently enacted. There appears to be no sense of time attached to the vision. Induced clairvoyance is, in effect, nothing more than the faculty of natural clairvoyance brought into temporary activity by suitable excitation. The Crystal is a ready means of developing clairvoyance where a tendency to it is known to exist. Quartz or beryl seems to induce clairvoyance in some people. The fact that it does not act similarly upon all subjects seems to indicate that the difference is not in its action but in the predisposition of the subject. For some people, a black concave mirror induces hallucinations. For some others, a bowl of water has been found effective as a medium in some cases. The degree of sensibility to stimulus of this kind differs with the subject. There are some in whom the psychic faculties are more active than in others. In some, these powers are hereditary, in others, they are developed by an innate tendency, aided by favouring circumstances. In most persons, the natural powers take a more practical turn, making them successful in mundane affairs rather than in those that are psychic and spiritual. The visions are in the subconscious mind or soul of the seer; but the mirror serves as a medium for visualizing the impressions which come up before the mind's eye, and produce inhibition of the basilar portion of the brain through the optic thalami, thus placing the attentive mind in a passive condition.

## Conclusion

I have listed some of the occult practices that are common among the general public. Many people out of curiosity are drawn towards them. Some of them can be fun. However, a person with a high degree of suggestibility may be programmed by the words of the occult practitioner. Many of the effects of the occult practices are the result of the power of suggestion. Once a suggestion is made, the customer may believe in it and proceed to make it happen. So, dabbling in occult practices can lead a person to destruction.

## Endnotes

[1] 1 Samuel 28:7-19

[2] *Carpenter, William Benjamin (12 March 1852). "On the influence of suggestion in modifying and directing muscular movement, independently of volition". Proceedings of the Royal Institution of Great Britain. The Royal Institution: 147–153*

[3] https://en.wikipedia.org/wiki/Automatic_writing

[4] https://en.wikipedia.org/wiki/Automatic_writing

[5] https://en.wikipedia.org/wiki/Automatic_writing

[6] *The Oxford English Dictionary*, 2nd ed., Oxford University Press, 1998.

[7] https://en.wikipedia.org/wiki/Tarot, accessed on 2/2/2016

[8] Brigit, "What is Tarot and How does it Work?" http://www.biddytarot.com/what-is-tarot-how-does-it-work/, accessed on 30/1/2016

[9] http://www.biddytarot.com/what-is-tarot-how-does-it-work/, accessed on 30/1/2016

[10] http:/ en.wikipedia.org/wiki/ Western Astrology, (accessed on January 15th, 2016)

[11] Ibid.

[12] http:/ en.wikipedia.org/wiki/ History of Astrology

[13] http:/ en.wikipedia.org/wiki/ Western Astrology

[14] http:/ en.wikipedia.org/wiki/ Western Astrology

[15] Montague Summers, *Geography of Witchcraft* (New York: Kessinger books Limited, 2003), 67

[16] Ibid, 54.

[17] Moody, R.A, Life after life, Covington, GA, Mockingbird, 1975

[18] Olaf Blanke and Sebastian Dieguez, Leaving Body and Life Behind: Out-of-Body and Near-Death Experience p.323 (The Neurology of Consciousness

[19] http://www.pewresearch.org/fact-tank/2015/10/30/18-of-americans-say-theyve-seen-a-ghost/

[20] http://www.awakeninthedream.com/catching-the-bug-of-synchronicity/

# Chapter 6

# The Place of the Occult in Various Worldviews

Aworldview is the comprehensive framework of one's basic beliefs about things and their relationships. It is the basic perspective we use to understand the world around us and our experience of it. It is an everyday ordinary-language description of the world that shapes and guides our lives, helping us to explore, understand and explain the world around us and everything in it, and how things are all related to each other, by giving us a way in which we can see them. It is a set of presuppositions which we hold consciously or unconsciously about the basic make up of our world. To believe that something is impossible is to deny its existence. The mind pays no attention to what it has denied and builds up its image of the world from the limited realities it has accepted as `possible.'. This image is necessarily restricted not by what exists, but by what the mind declares exists. When this way of perceiving the world is used for theologizing or creating scientific theories, it restricts the scope of both theology and science. Anthropologists show that different cultures have different sensory worlds. Selective screening of sensory data admits some things while filtering others, so that experiences as it is perceived through one set of cultural patterns which is quite different from the experiences perceived through another. Our world-view is constructed from the totality of our life experiences. It is made up of womb and birth experiences, of our formative years, of interactions with parents and others, genetic sensitivities and insensitivities, physical and cultural circumstances, linguistic environments, education and so on. It is a prevailing myth within which we live.

Our worldview, our inherited representation of the world is related to our mother-tongue and the environment in which we grow up. It varies from culture to culture. Part of the difficulty in recognizing another worldview resides in the way cultures exploit our proneness to `sensory repression'. For example, cultures can build in the mind screens that usually remain out of the awareness of the individual. Anthropologists show that different cultures have different sensory worlds. Selective screening of sensory data admits some things while filtering others, so that experiences as it is perceived through one set of culturally patterns sensory screens is quite different from the experiences perceived through another.

Anthropology has taught us that the world is differently defined in different places. The very metaphysical presuppositions differ, space does not concern to Euclidean geometry, time does not form a continuous unidirectional flow, causation does not conform to Aristotelian logic, man is not differentiated from non-man or life from death as in our world. The central importance of entering worlds other than our own lies in the fact that the experience leads us to understand that our world is also a cultural construct. A question determines and brings about its answer just as the desired and shapes the nature of the kind of the question asked.

Thomas Kuhn's influential book, *the Structure of scientific revolutions*, maintains that both theories and data in science are dependent on the prevailing paradigms of the scientific community. He defined a paradigm as a cluster of conceptual, metaphysical, and methodological presuppositions embodied in a tradition of scientific work. With a new paradigm, the old data are reinterpreted and seen in new ways, and new kinds of data are sought. A paradigm shift is, in Kuhn's words, "a radical transformation of the scientific imagination", a 'scientific revolution' which is not the product of experiment alone.[1] In the choice between paradigms, there are no rules for applying scientific criteria or for judging their relative importance. Their evaluation is an act of judgment by the scientific community. A paradigm defines a community which works together within a set of shared assumptions. An established paradigm is resistant to falsifications, since discrepancies between theory and data can be set aside as anomalies or reconciled by introducing ad hoc hypotheses.[2]

Quantum Physics tells us that observers cannot observe without altering what they see. An observer and the observed are interrelated in a fundamental sense. The exact nature of this interrelation is not clear, but there is a growing body of evidence that the distinction between the 'in here'[1] and the 'out there' is an illusion. A question determines and brings about its answer just as the desired answer shapes the nature of the kind of the question asked. What we experience is not external reality, but our interaction with it. This is the fundamental assumption of 'complementarity.' Complementarity is the concept developed by Niels Bohr to explain the wave-particle duality of light. Wave-like characteristics and particle-like characteristics are mutually exclusive or complementary aspects of light. Although one of them always excludes the other, because light or anything else, cannot be both wave-like and particle-like at the same time. How can mutually exclusive wave-like and particle-like behaviors both be properties of one and the same light? They are properties of our interaction with light. Depending upon our choice of experiment, we can cause light to manifest either particle-like properties or wavelike properties.

All systems limp. There is no way of describing the world, no world-view is complete. All leave out a part of what it means to be human. If a worldview provides nourishment and fulfillment to one part of our feature, it leaves out or disregards other parts as unreal. Each worldview, furthermore, includes as one of its major premises the concept that it is the only valid way of being in the world and that the others are not valid. We are constantly tempted, therefore, to accept only one system we were raised on, and thus to feel only a part of our being. In human history the other parts almost invariably remain undernourished and wither.

## a.     Shamanistic and Magical Worldview and the Occult

Magic has always been about control. It is about control over the environment, over other humans, over knowledge, over fate, over the self. Magic was a vast spectrum of thought and action about the world, whose practices were inextricably entangled with the disciplines that we now call religion, philosophy, medicine and natural science. The border between religion and magic has always been porous. Magic is the attempt by man to gain control over the world of man, nature, and the supernatural. In magic, man attempts to become god over all things and to assert his power and control over all reality.

Magic thus becomes a religion in as much as it is attached to controlling reality through the control of Idols.

Shamanism is a notion used to describe a pattern of ritual behavior and belief in which charismatic individuals deliberately enter an altered state of consciousness in order to interact with various spirits for the benefit of community. First and foremost, the shaman performs the crucial role of mediator between his or her community and the spirit world including nature, ensuring equilibrium between the two. This includes such activities as divining the cause of an illness or auguring the future and acting as a guide for the souls of the dead to ensure their passage to the spirit realm. The shaman may call the spirits to interact with the community during a séance, acting as the medium for this interaction. As a community's healer, the shaman also deals with matters concerning the community as a social unit and maintains their sacred myths and traditions. Primitive tribal people believed that the world was full of unseen forces. The magical powers are a part of this underground world: powers of second sight, prevision, telepathy, and divination.

This is how Mircea Eliade defines a Shaman: "Ethnologists have fallen into the habit of using the terms shaman, medicine man, sorcerer, and magician interchangeably to designate certain individuals possessing magico-religious powers found in all primitive societies. The shaman is the great master of ecstasy."[3] All through the primitive and modern worlds we find individuals who profess to maintain relations with spirits, whether they control them or are possessed by them. . Principal function of the shaman in Central and North Asia is magical healing, and divination and clairvoyance are part of the shaman's mystical techniques.

Shamanistic altered state of consciousness is predominantly induced through the ritualised consumption of psychoactive substances, although other methods may also be used. These include fasting, physical and mental deprivation, torture, lack of sleep, ceaseless dancing and rhythmic activities such as drumming and chanting. The psychoactive substances used to induce trance may include psilocybin, hallucinogenic mushrooms, peyote, datura, opium, ergot, cannabis, coca and ayahuasca.

When Shamanism becomes a means of control, it is like magic. Magic is the attempt by man to gain control over the world of man, nature, and the supernatural. In magic, man attempts to become god over all things and to assert his power and control over all reality. Magic thus becomes a religion in as much as it is attached to controlling reality through the control of idols and symbols.

Shamanism, as practiced in various tribes around the world, differs drastically from one another. The worldview of the Shamans and the magicians can be summarized from the Hermetical principles. Hermeticism, is a religious, philosophical, and esoteric tradition based primarily upon writings attributed to Hermes Trismegistus. His teachings are codified in a book called the Kybalion in 1908.[4] His writings have greatly influenced the Western esoteric tradition and were considered to be of great importance during the Renaissance and the Reformation. Much of the importance of Hermeticism arises from its connection with the development of science during the time from 1300 to 1600 AD. The prominence that it gave to the idea of influencing or controlling nature led many scientists to look to magic and its allied arts such as alchemy, astrology which, it was thought, could put Nature to test by means of experiments. The Seven Hermetic Principles upon which the entire Hermetic Philosophy is based, are as follows:[5]

1. The Principle of Mentalism: "ALL IS MIND; The Universe is Mental."-- Everything that exists is spirit.

2. The Principle of Correspondence: *As Above, So Below; As Within, So Without; As the Universe, So the Soul.* It basically means that everything is connected and is in correspondence.

3. The Principle of Vibration: This Principle embodies the truth that "everything is in motion;" "everything vibrates;" "nothing is at rest;" facts which Modern Science endorses, and which each new scientific discovery tends to verify. This principle explains the difference between the different manifestations of matter and spirit.

4. The Principle of Polarity: This Principle embodies the truth that "everything is dual;" "everything has two poles;" "everything has its pair of opposites. Take, for example, love and hate. They are the same thing, but different degrees.

5. The Principle of Rhythm: This Principle embodies the truth that in everything, there is manifested a measured motion, to and fro, a swing backward and forward, a high-tide and a low-tide.

6. The Principle of Cause and Effect: This Principle embodies the fact that there is a Cause for every Effect; an Effect from every Cause.

7. The Principle of Gender: This Principle embodies the truth that there is GENDER manifested in everything--the Masculine and the Feminine Principles ever at work.

Shamanistic practices are based on some of these principles. So, when the Shamans and magicians believe in their rituals and go into altered states of consciousness, they experience control over their realities. People who believe in them also experience those realities.

## 2.   Scientific Worldviews and the Occult

What is commonly called the scientific world-view was born during the European Enlightenment period of the 17th and 18th centuries. Often called a scientific world-view, it affirms that what is real is that which can be known by science, namely, the space-time world of matter and energy and how it operates.

In the last 500 years, materialistic philosophy has permeated every level of society. So pervasive has it been that most people in one way or another have come under its influence. This fundamental materialistic philosophy arose from an understanding of the universe which was based on a mechanistic model. Scientific materialism makes two assertions: (1) the scientific method is the only reliable path to knowledge; (2) matter is the fundamental reality in the universe.

Newton built an understating of the universe, which was so successful that until the present century it was accepted by all scientists. He wanted to explain all-natural phenomena in mathematical mechanics.[6] For Newton matter was extended in space, and reality consisted of concrete objects moving in space and time. Measurement of mass, motion and other properties, and their interrelationships, provided the model of the universe.

Biological science went ahead to attempt to explain life and living phenomena in terms of mechanical causality, using the concepts of physics and chemistry. Darwin enunciated the theory of evolution. Molecular biology has made extraordinary discoveries about the nature and function of genetic material, and in the area of genetic engineering, revolutionary new technologies have opened, all within the framework of this mechanistic system. Life itself then came to be explained exclusively in terms of mechanistic philosophy. In cosmology and the natural sciences generally, the existence of God was no longer necessary. In psychology the existence of a soul was considered superfluous. The whole human being could be explained in terms of mechanistic causality.

The mechanistic philosophy led to the mechanistic view of life. Here, all the living beings, including humans, were machines that were much more complicated. This view influenced the physician's attitude towards health and illness. The mechanisation of human life resulted in the deification of humans and their powers to know the world. Reason became the undisputed light that would eventually dispel all darkness. Science became an all-powerful tool in the hands of modern humans, with which humankind could understand the language of the universe, and even manipulate it to suit its own needs, and thus play the God of the universe. Hence, one can see how the will-to-power flowered as the technocracy of the modern age.

The Industrial Revolution changed the world in dramatic ways. Scientific and technological development has deeply affected manners and customs as well as minds. Railways first, and then automobiles, allowed people to travel faster and faster, farther and farther.

Information is a major issue in almost every corner of the world. We now have the Internet. Never were people able to communicate, work and even play with so many different people at the same time all over the world. This *is* the great cultural revolution. Everything can be found or accomplished thanks to the Web: shopping, learning, and even exploring new countries without leaving one's armchair! Culture can be and is being electronically transmitted.

## 3.   Quantum Age Worldview

In the recent past, new wrinkles were added to our understanding of the universe: Quantum mechanics, the Uncertainty Principle, String theory, dark matter, Higg's particle, black holes, expanding universe, and Relativity, to name a few. With the emergence of quantum computing, processing power of computers is increasing at a tremendous pace, helping humans to solve highly complex problems with the help of intelligent and more powerful data-crunching machines.

New digital technologies such as quantum computing, artificial intelligence and robotics, cloud computing, Internet of Things, 3D Printing, cryptocurrencies, big data analytics, virtual reality, augmented reality, autonomous vehicles, sensor technologies, etc. are emerging, and they are transforming organizations and human lives in more radical ways than ever before. From robotic surgery to using robots on the shop-floor and even in restaurants, robots are replacing humans in repetitive mechanical tasks and even in dangerous situations. Robots are used extensively by Amazon in their fulfillment centers. Future wars will be in cyberspace, and on the ground, robotic armies will replace the human army for most purposes. In the air, unmanned robot-controlled or remote-controlled drones will carry lethal weapons into enemy territory.

On the positive front, problem solving based on Artificial Intelligence and other digital technologies may lead to replacement of professionals such as doctors, lawyers, and other professionals. Machine Learning and Deep Learning are outpacing the limits of human reasoning and thinking. With the increasing use of Artificial Intelligence and machine learning, the role of humans will shift more to areas that require judgment, creativity, empathy, and collaboration, while using these techniques to enhance human capacity. Artificial Intelligence machines could be working alongside humans in many professions and industries such as manufacturing, warehousing, medicine, aviation, law, military defense, and space exploration. Many of them could even replace humans. We are seeing a new awakening and the emergence of a new digital culture.

The advent of the development of the field of quantum physics is ushering in a paradigm shift in understanding of our world. This paradigm shift has led many physicists to re-examining their scientific understanding of their beliefs, regarding the nature of the universe and how it truly operates. In addition, this has created cognitive dissonance among physicists as to how to translate and integrate this new scientific knowledge and understanding into present day teaching and research activities. This new scientific model has also been examined by theologians who have identified the similarities and commonalities between quantum physics, theology and a spirituality associated with the worship of a deity. The current innovative blending of contemporary spirituality and quantum physics supports their transformative integration into a non-dualistic, holistic system of theory and application.

The foundation of the discipline known as Quantum Physics rests upon the work of Max Planck that led to the revision of scientific thought and theory, regarding the existence of energy in the form of distinct packets called "quanta" that are nonreductionistic in nature. The work of Albert Einstein in 1905, establishing the existence of the photon and the photoelectric effect, were other scientific achievements of significant importance in the field of quantum physics. Other contributors to the scientific and theoretical foundations for quantum physics include Erwin Schrodinger, Werner Heisenberg, Neils Bohr and Wolfgang Pauli. Their contributions helped to advance the theoretical basis for quantum physics. It is interesting to note that each of these researchers were also aware of the deeper spiritual aspects of quantum physics even though they were classically trained physicists.

Contemporary quantum physics utilizes mathematics to elucidate the relationship between the observer and research events in which the observer influences the processes being observed that alters the outcome of the research in the expected directions of the observer. The current focus of quantum physics development includes a variety of theoretical investigations into the contemporary aspects of quantum physics that have evolved from scientific inquiry and research activity. These areas include "wave particle duality, quantum tunneling, quantum entanglement, quantum optics, electrodynamics, unified field theory, black body radiation, photoelectric effect, causality, superstring theory, and dark matter." These specialized areas of professional inquiry indicate that substantial strides have been made in the field of quantum physics that have resulted in the identification of salient theoretical aspects that heretofore were unknown.

The principle of entanglement has baffled scientists. Entanglement is what Einstein referred to as 'spooky action at a distance'. The theory holds that when two atoms have been intrinsically associated, they remain linked despite physical separation. We understand that nothing in our physical universe exceeds light speed (including signals or information using a physical means). Yet, if you change the state of one entangled particle, this is mirrored by an instantaneous change in the state of the other entangled particle/s. The 'instantaneous' should have tweaked your interest. The communication between these particles not only exceeds the speed of light, it happens in exact synchronicity, regardless of any intervening distance. There is no direct cause and effect in play on both particles; change one particle's state and you instantly change the states of all other particles, entangled with that particle. Along with this theory of entanglement, we have another theory that the observer affects the observed.

Occult and parapsychological phenomena cannot be accounted for using the four fundamental forces of Physics: Gravitational force, Electromagnetic force, the weak force and the Strong Nuclear force. So, in the scientific worldviews, there is no place for the occult.

## 4.    The Holographic Worldview[7] and the Occult

In the mid-1960's, Holography was developed, in which the interference patterns of twin laser beams create realistic three-dimensional images. Any fragment of the holographic film can be used to create the entire original 3-D image. What is fascinating about the hologram is that if the photographic plate on which the object is recorded is cut into pieces, each piece when illuminated by coherent light will reconstruct the whole image, perfect in every detail, although less sharply defined. The hologram is a concrete example of the principle that the whole is present in every part.

If a hologram of a rose is cut in half and then illuminated by a laser, each half will still be found to contain the entire image of the rose. Indeed, even if the halves are divided again, each snippet of film will always be found to contain a smaller but intact version of the original image. Unlike normal photographs, every part of a hologram contains all the information possessed by the whole. The "whole in every part" nature of a hologram provides us with an entirely new way of understanding organization and order. The new physics presents us with an understanding of the physical world as a field of energies, an integrated whole in which the whole is present in every part.

Each of us, in the cells of our body, is linked with the original matter of the universe because the entire universe, and everything in it, is one integrated whole. We are all linked with all the original cells which began to form on this earth as it reached a state when life could emerge. The status of the observer in science has also been reconsidered. The earlier accounts had identified objectivity with the separability of the observer from the object of observation. But in quantum physics the influence of the process of observation on the system observed is crucial. In relativity, the most basic measurements, such as the mass, velocity and length of an object, depend on the frame of reference of the observer.

In addition to its phantom like nature, such a universe would possess other rather startling features. If the apparent separateness of subatomic particles is illusory, it means that at a deeper level of reality all things in the universe are infinitely interconnected. The electrons in a carbon atom in the human brain are connected to the subatomic particles that comprise every salmon that swims, every heart that beats, and every star that shimmers in the sky. Everything interpenetrates everything, and although human nature may seek to categorize and pigeonhole and subdivide, the various phenomena of the universe, all apportionments are of necessity artificial and all of nature is ultimately a seamless web.

In a holographic universe, even time and space could no longer be viewed as fundamentals. Because concepts such as location break down in a universe in which nothing is truly separate from anything else, time and three-dimensional space would also have to be viewed as projections of this deeper order. At its deeper level reality is a sort of super hologram in which the past, present, and future all exist simultaneously.

In this Holographic worldview, all objects and events are perceived as related to the total Universe. Each entity is separate enough to be able to be aware of its own wishes. In this worldview intercessory prayer is possible. Here I can say 'When I pray, coincidences start to happen when I don't pray, they don't happen.[1] In intercessory prayer, the part (the universe, the person) attempts to bring the great forces of the whole (the universe, God, nature) to the aid and repair of another part that is perceived as damaged. Usually this is done by a trained single-mindedness of prayer, a total one-pointing of the total part to get the signal, the -wish, through to the whole. In the materialistic world-view intercessory prayer is non-sense. There is simply no way it can work. The basic limiting principles of the Holographic world-view are:

1.  Each object, entity, or event is a separate unity, but has no clear demarcation line with the organic integral unity that makes up reality.

2. There are tremendous forces in the cosmos that can sometimes be harnessed to bear on a local part or situation.

3. These can be harnessed by an absolute single mindedness or purpose of any conscious part of the system.

4. Space is real and 'exists' but is totally unimportant. Parts of the whole are separated by it, but since they are also connected through being parts of the same One, this does not matter.

5. Knowledge of other parts can come from two sources: a» From observation, as in the sensory modes.

a. from observation, as in the sensory modes.

b. through being a part of the whole and perceiving other parts through the whole.

6. From the viewpoint the individual part, there is a free will of each sentient part. From the view point of the whole, all actions that parts will take are decided and their results recorded.

7. Since whatever is done to one part affects the whole, an ethical principle is built into the universe. If one part moves another toward greater harmony with the whole, all the whole - including the part that took the action - benefits. If one part moves to disrupt the harmony (hurt it, damage it, and stunt its becoming) between another part and the whole, the disruption affects the whole including the part that took the action.

8. Valid information need not be only through the sense.

9. The law of causality can be transcended.

10. The flow of time need not be linear.

11. There is a certain 'consciousness' in matter.

Today, we are becoming increasingly aware that we live in a dynamically inter-related universe. The universe seems to be an evolving network of relationships. The cosmic web appears to be alive. It moves, grows and changes continuously. The Newtonian notions of absolute space and time have been challenged by the theory of special relativity of Einstein. Space is nothing apart from the things that exist. Similarly, the view that absolute time flows from infinite past into infinite future, the same everywhere in the universe without any relation to the events that happen, has been shown to be incorrect. There is no time apart from change. Thus, neither space nor time has an existence outside the system of evolving relationships that comprise the universe. The quantum theory maps the dynamic of the micro-physical world. At the macro-level, quantum effects seem to be invisible. But at the micro-level the quantum effects are highly appreciable. In the light of mass-energy equivalence, as taught by the special theory of relativity, mass could no longer be identified with the indestructible stuff which was thought to make all things. Mass came to be understood as a form of energy that as such can be transformed into other forms of energy.

The Holographic worldview may be able to accept the occult and parapsychological phenomena. But it does not explain how.

## 5.   Vibrational Worldview and the Occult

Everything in our material universe is vibrating; the earth under our feet, the water we drink, the plants in the forest, animals and ourselves, even our thoughts. If it exists, it vibrates. And all vibrations radiate outward in waves. Everything has its own vibrational frequency - the table, the car, the rock and even our thoughts and feelings. A chair may look solid and still, but within the chair are millions of subatomic particles and in each atom, the electrons are moving nearly at the speed of light. In Fig 1, the structure of the atom is shown. The chair is pure energy and movement. However, we cannot see it, so it appears separate and solid to us. It is an illusion.

Following is a table, showing roughly the rates of vibration which each of our senses can perceive.

| Attribute | Vibrations per second |
|---|---|
| Touch | 1 to 16 |
| Sound | 16 to 20,000 |
| Electromagnetic | 16,000 to 540 million |
| Microwave | 250 million to 2,75,000 million |
| Heat or infrared | 250,000 to250,000,000 million |
| Visible light | 250,000,000 million to 1125,000,000 million |
| Ultraviolet | 125,000,000 million to 60,000,000,000 million |
| X-ray | 60,000,000,000 million to 4611000000000 million |

*Table 1: Frequency Table*

There is no solidity in the universe. A form that appears solid is created by an underlying vibration. Vibrations express themselves in corresponding geometrical figures and in this way build up crystals that are the expressions of vibration. Crystals collectively form a body of an element according to its vibration. The forms of snowflakes and faces of flowers take on their shape, because they are responding to some sound in nature.

Looking at the structure of the atom as seen in Fig.1, we see that the electrons around the nucleus are moving nearly at the speed of light. This means that all inert matter is full of movement which is invisible to our eyes.

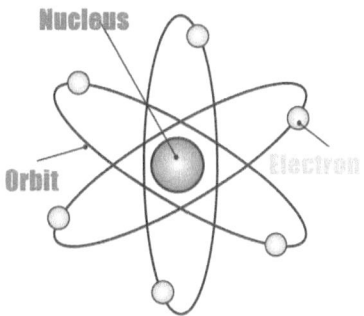

*Fig. 1: Structure of an Atom*

Frequency can be expressed in many ways. However, at its core it is an expression of energy. This energy expresses itself in wave forms, but at its core it is actually made of cyclic patterns of scalar waves (standing waves) that flash "on" and "off," causing it to pop in and out of existence. If we only look at frequency as a wave, then the definition of it would be the number of waves that pass a fixed point in a time cycle. For example, if it takes 1/2 of a second for a wave to pass a fixed point in a time cycle, the frequency would be 2 per second.

The true state of reality is made of energy that flashes on and off, creating energy codes and frequency patterns that are processed by our consciousness to give us the perception of time and the solidity of matter. In other words, matter behaves more like an illusion. However, from our perspective, this "illusion" is very real, and is necessary to help us to evolve so that we should take it very seriously.

Frequency gives matter uniqueness and characteristics, so that when the consciousness of our mind and body processes the energy patterns of an object, we see shapes, colors and textures. The combination of frequency, vibration and oscillation are some of the major energy properties that organize matter into sacred geometries, giving matter "life" and the ability to structure itself into objects.

## Resonance

If a tuning fork, designed to produce a frequency of 256 cycles a second, is sounded anywhere near another fork with the same natural frequency, the second one will begin to vibrate gently in sympathy with the first, even without being touched. Energy has been transferred from one to the other. A flashing light of the same frequency as a brain rhythm produces resonance and alarming effects even though the flicker may be too fast for us to see.

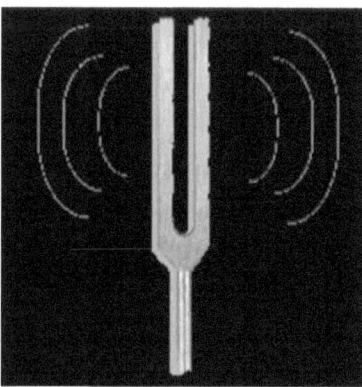

*Fig. 2: Vibrating Tuning Fork*

The idea of 'shape' having an influence on the functions taking place within it is not a new one. The fermenting action is enhanced in certain shapes than in others. Healing takes place better in certain shapes. Schizophrenic patients improve better in trapezoidal hospital wards. It is possible that all shapes have their own qualities and that the forms we see around us are the result of combinations of environmental frequencies.

Form is a function of frequency. Can magic words and sacred formulas and chants in fact exert an influence that differs from other sounds chosen at random? Sounds and words do have different physical properties. If resonance can be produced between an air column in a sender's throat and another in a receiver's ear, then similar transfers of energy can take place between the throat and other parts of the environment. When Joshua's people shouted with a great shout, the walls of Jericho fell (Josh6/20). The sudden loud cry of a Samurai swordsman breaks the nerve of an adversary.

We are all sensitive to the physical forces around us and it is possible to enhance this sensitivity. One such sensitivity is the water divining ability. Many animals have an extraordinary sensitivity to water, and some such as the elephant succeed in finding it underground. In times of drought, elephants often perform vital community services by using tusks and pile-driving feet to expose hidden water sources. Like the surface of the earth, two thirds of most animals are water. One of the preconditions for resonance is that there should be similar, or at least compatible structures in the sender and the receiver, so if the energy is broadcast by a water source, it could probably find a response in the body of most mammals. The literature abounds with accounts of dowsers locating missing persons, criminals, and dead bodies by following the indications of a sensitized rod.

The choice of a resting place naturally must be made very carefully regarding warmth and shelter and safety from predators, but often an animal will choose a place that seems to be far less appealing on these grounds than another only a short distance away. Domestic dogs and cats show the same behaviour and their owners know full well that it is no good making this decision on the pet's behalf – they must wait until the animal chooses its own place and then put the sleeping basket there. There are some places on which an animal will not lie on any account.

Every part of our body vibrates to its own rhythm. The brain has a unique set of brain waves. In neuroscience, there are five distinct brain wave frequencies, namely Beta, Alpha, Theta, Delta and the lesser known Gamma. Each frequency, measured in cycles per second (Hz), has its own set of characteristics, representing a specific level of brain activity and hence, a unique state of consciousness.

Some of the occult phenomena can be explained using this paradigm. Every person has a vibrational frequency. As it happens in resonance, energy can be transferred for healing to another person when they are in resonance. 'Slaying in the spirit' may happen because of the frequency difference between two people. Possession and exorcism may also have something to do with frequencies.

## Endnotes

[1] Thomas Kuhn, The structure of Scientific revolutions, University of Chicago press, 1970, p.172

[2] Thomas Kuhn, The structure of Scientific revolutions, University of Chicago press, 1970, p.78

[3] Mircea Eliade, Shamanism ,Archaic Techniques of Ecstasy Translated from the French by Willard r. Trask Princeton university press, 1953, p.23

[4] http://www.sacred-texts.com/eso/kyb/kyb04.htm

[5] The Kyballion, Chapter 2, Yogi publication society, 1908

[6] E.A. Burtt, The Metaphysical Foundations of Modern Science, Double Day Anchor Books, 1954, p.211-212

[7] P T Joseph, Faith Process and Human Development, Jnana Deepa, Vol 17, No.1, 20014 p.97

# Conclusion

## The Place of the Supernatural and the Occult in Christianity

The most consistent characteristic of a person's worldview is that it is acquired unknowingly without any real effort. It is simply the core beliefs of a person or group of people that determine the decisions that they make about life. These decisions may range from (1) the trivial, for example, what one will have for dinner, to (2) the more significant, for example, what area of work will be one's life vocation, or to (3) the ultimate questions of life and death and eternity. This acquisition of a world view is almost as true for the Christian as them of the other faiths. One's positions are just a product of unquestioned acceptance of what others have said or what feels "good" or "right" now. Certainly, one's world view will change as the person reflects more and learns about other world views and that in turn will modify one's own world view.

Modern Christianity suffers from two serious shortcomings when it comes to the supernatural world. First, many Christians claim to believe in the supernatural but think and live like sceptics. They find talk of the supernatural world uncomfortable. The other shortcoming is that Christianity is bending under the weight of its own rationalism, a modern worldview that would be foreign to the biblical writers. Traditional Christian teaching has kept the unseen world at arm's length in the recent past. We believe in the Godhead because there's no point to Christianity without it. The rest of the unseen world is handled with scepticism. Those two shortcomings, while seemingly quite different, are born of the same fundamental, underlying problem: Their view of the unseen world isn't framed by the ancient worldview of the biblical writers.

The Christian worldview is more than a religious belief system. In fact, the Christian worldview is a complete and integrated framework through which to see the entire world. The major themes of a biblical worldview are: Creation, fall, redemption, and consummation. These themes are not simply chronological, although that is part of the structure of Scripture.

The beginning of a Christian worldview is in God's creation of the universe, as explicitly taught in the book of Genesis and confessed in the Apostles' Creed, "We believe in God the Father Almighty, Maker of heaven and earth." The central affirmation of Scripture is not only that there is a God, but that God has acted and spoken in history. Even though men and women are created in God's image, the entrance of sin into the world has had great and negative influences upon God's creation, especially humans created in God's image. At the core of a Christian worldview is the foundational truth that Jesus Christ's life, death, and resurrection have brought about redemption from sin.

A Christian worldview becomes a driving force in life to those who believe, giving us a sense of God's plan and purpose for this world. It provides a framework for ethical living. It has implications for understanding history. God who has acted in history in past events will also act in history to consummate this age. It offers a new way of thinking, seeing, and doing, based on a new way of being. A Christian worldview offers meaning and purpose for all aspects of life.

The Christian life is supernatural. It is a life lived by the power of the Holy Spirit. Without the Holy Spirit and the power, He provides the Christian life is impossible. Any attempt to exclude the power of God will result in nothing more than a human religion based on the power and cleverness of human ability. It makes human beings the source of power instead of God. St. Paul explained it this way: "I have been crucified with Christ. It is no longer I who live, but Christ who lives in me. And the life I now live in the flesh I live by the faith of the Son of God, who loved me and gave himself for me". To live in Christ, we must be willing to die in Christ. We have been crucified with Him and His life must replace ours and the life we live is lived by His faith.

St. Paul did not want the people he taught to think that the Christian life was one that people can initiate and manipulate. He wrote to the Corinthians, "My speech and my preaching were not in persuasive words of wisdom, but in demonstration of the Spirit and of power, that your faith might not rest in the wisdom of men but in the power of God." In other words, St. Paul did not lean on his human ability to persuade others through words and wisdom but chose instead to allow the Holy Spirit and His power to be expressed. He wanted people to set their eyes on the power of God rather than human ability and power. Many today want to bring Christianity down to the level of human ability. That is the devastating mistake that many Christians make. Many popular teachers are asserting that the supernatural aspects of the faith such as miracles and healings can be discounted. Making that claim relegates Christianity to nothing more than an academic exercise. The church is a supernatural, heavenly, God-infused body functioning on earth as the dwelling place of God and the living evidence of His existence and purpose. Even this truth cannot be perceived by human knowledge but, as Paul puts it, can only be known by enlightened hearts filled with the revelation and knowledge of Him.

## Scientific Worldview's Effect on Theology

Till recently, the model for theologizing was limited to a great extent by the worldview which became dominant in philosophy and science around the 18th century in Europe. That worldview assumes that we are shut up in a physical universe where no experience can reach us except through our senses, and therefore, it is absurd to imagine that we can perceive, know and act outside the ordinary operation of the senses. This is basically a materialistic and overly rationalistic way of viewing reality. During this period, Christian theology submitted to:

1. Demythologization approach of Rudolf Bultman and others.

2. The use of various reductionist- functionalist, psychological or sociological- theories which have been popular from Max Weber to Freud.

3. The relegation of all such phenomena to the category of superstition, folk-tale, fiction and saga which has characterized the work of many earlier historians, anthropologists and psychologists.

To some, it would simply seem philosophically illicit that parapsychologists, or anyone else for that matter, should attempt to ask questions concerning the reality of invisible influence in the life of mankind with empirical methods borrowed from the empirical sciences. Historians of religion and theologians alike seem to deal more comfortably with religious and philosophical questions on another level, quite apart from the whole question of the empirical verification of the reality or non-reality of the so-called paranormal phenomena. Thus, the demythologization process has become one of the popular intellectual approaches to questions of the paranormal by those who are concerned with the meaning of human religious experience within various cultural contexts. In the absence of factual knowledge about real Psi powers, and the universal phenomenology, the answers inevitably belong to the realm of private religious affirmations of the scholar as an individual rather than to the scientific study of religions.

According to the Biblical scholar, Bultmann, the New Testament worldview is what he calls 'a mythological world view,' and the one he believes all modern men necessarily hold, which he calls the 'modern scientific world view.' One of the most important ways the concept of world- man's notion of a world-view is to deny the possibility of just 'pick and choose' approach to the New Testament into the forms of a sweeping "either or not." One of the prime functions of Bultmann's notion of worldview is to deny the possibility of just 'pick and choose' approach to the New Testament beliefs. The reason is that the world-view theory says that the beliefs are not independent of one another but have at their basis a system of general beliefs about the world. All the beliefs imply the system with something like logical necessity: if you do not buy the system, you cannot have the beliefs. Under a term like 'mythical,' the choice has, of course, already been decided beforehand, and any modern man who dares to believe the New Testament will be regarded as having sacrificed his intellect, because of the mythological world-view he questions whether there is any truth at all in the New Testament:

> Man's knowledge and mastery of the world have advanced to such an extent through science that it is no longer possible for anyone seriously to hold the New Testament view of the world - in fact there is no one who does. "What meaning, for instance, can we attach to such phrases in the creed as 'descended into hell' or 'ascended into heaven'? We no longer believe in the three storied universe which the creeds take for granted. The only honest way of reciting the creeds is to strip the mythological framework from the truth they enshrine - that is, if they contain any truth at all, which is just the question that theology must ask. No one who is old enough to think for himself supposes that God lives in a local heaven. There is no longer any heaven in the traditional sense of the word.[1]

In the past, science and theology appear to have deliberately avoided each other with science being within the purview of man, and theology being within the purview of the clergy. And yet, there are instances of the interweaving of science with theology and spirituality throughout history. These events began with the on-going historical scientific developments of man in ancient civilizations that have subsequently contributed to our current prevailing scientific and spiritual beliefs and practices. Among the marvellous discoveries resulting from the scientific endeavours of quantum physicists are the concept of the quantum field and how the field operates in a manner like how theology views God as being all- knowing and all-omnipresent. The similarity of these two differing viewpoints elucidates the present seemingly daunting task that both quantum physicists and theological and spiritual leaders have before them.

The combination of spirituality and quantum physics appears to be an unlikely non-dualistic based possibility. According to the dualistic approach, the believers in God and spirituality posit a deistic view of the universe in comparison to the diametric beliefs that are espoused by the non-deistic scientific, theory and research-based believers. These understandings indicate the existence of two very different views and beliefs regarding the origin of the universe and mankind and the resulting worldview each group holds. The non-dualistic approach to understanding the universe combines these two diverse approaches into a single comprehensive system of beliefs that incorporate God, science and spirituality into one philosophical, theoretical and dynamic system.

One aspect of the New Testament narrative which has been discredited almost universally in modern times is the belief in the realm of spiritual beings, a vast realm of angelic and demonic beings. Along with the belief in spiritual healing, dreams, visions and other such intrusions into our self-contained physical world, the idea of active and effective spiritual entities is regarded as absurd. There is not much point in discussing discernment of spirits unless there is a spiritual world to discern. If we are indeed confined to the everyday world of space and time, talking about spiritual influences is quite nonsensical. If one is going to try to distinguish which influences come from God and which come from some other source, it is first necessary to believe that there is a spiritual world and that it affects our world profoundly.

## Charisms

The Spirit of God is the principal agent of the whole of the Church's mission. The Holy Spirit imparts special graces, or charisms, for the benefit of the whole Body of the Church.

Each member of the Church is gifted with these charisms, whether they are extraordinary, rooted in natural talents, or imparted for ministerial office. The charisms are exceedingly effective in meeting the needs within the Church (ad intra) and in empowering her mission to the world (ad extra). Included among the evident signs of hope today is the greater attentiveness of the Church to the voice of the Spirit through the charisms. The Church seeks a renewed appreciation of the Spirit as the principal agent of mission, of evangelization, as the one who builds the Kingdom of God within the course of history and prepares the world for full salvation in Jesus Christ.

In the synagogue in Capernaum, Jesus proclaimed his mission as follows:

> The spirit of the Lord is upon me; therefore, he has anointed me. He has sent me to bring glad tidings to the poor, to proclaim liberty to the captives, recovery of sight to the blind, and release to prisoners, to announce a year of favour from the Lord.

On the day of Pentecost, the Holy Spirit suddenly descended on the Lord's disciples in power ... like a strong, driving wind. "Tongues as of fire appeared which parted and came to rest on each of them. All were filled with the Holy Spirit". Charisms were manifested in the Church for the first time: "They began to express themselves in foreign tongues" and make bold proclamations as the Spirit prompted them.

What are the charisms? "*A charism is a special gift, a perceptible and freely bestowed manifestation of the Holy Spirit, a particular grace of God which is given for the benefit of the whole Body of the Church.*" At least 27 gifts are listed in scripture references covering a broad range of gifts, from prophecy and healing to mercy, teaching, almsgiving, perseverance, joy, encouragement, hospitality and leadership. St. Paul lists nine examples of the Spirit's manifestations as given in 1Cor 12:4-11.

Gifts of Grace: The power to speak, sometimes called Word Gifts: *Prophecy, Tongues, Interpretation of Tongues.*

Gifts of Service: The power to know: *Wisdom, Knowledge, And Discernment.* These gifts are the ability to express and understand various aspects of God's nature or plan in a matter that brings

Gifts of Works: The power to do: *Faith, Miracles, Healing.* Jesus' preaching was always accompanied by cures, miracles and deliverance that led the people to faith and enabled them to experience as well as hear the good news.

Charismatic gifts are as important to the Church today as they were in apostolic times. These gifts work to bring unity, to empower and to serve the Church's needs. The Church has declared: "Whether these charisms are very remarkable or simpler and widely diffused, they are to be received with thanksgiving and consolation since they are fitting and useful for the needs of the church."

A charism is a freely bestowed gift or Grace of God. So, one doesn't earn the charisms. The charisms are not bestowed as rewards for individual sanctity or holiness; rather, as gifts of God, the charisms are lavished on the people of God, the Church, as gift, initiated by God. The charisms strengthen the faith, hope, and love of her individual members. For example, one might *experience* charismatic activity within the Church and in that experience be confronted with the power and reality of God. A charism is a manifestation of the Holy Spirit given for the common good. As gratuitous manifestations of the Holy

Spirit, the charisms are clearly not possessions. They are to be used for the building up of the community.

Before the ascension, the Lord Jesus commissioned the apostles to preach the gospel to every creature and to baptize all who believe. He said: "*Signs like these will accompany those who have professed their faith: In my name they will drive out demons, they will speak new languages. They will pick up serpents with their hands, and if they drink any deadly thing, it will not harm them. They will lay hands on the sick, and they will recover.*"

The charism of prophecy is a manifestation of the Holy Spirit in which God communicates to his people, through his people, in human language, written, spoken, sung, or signed. Prophecy can be expressed through Scripture. Prophecy very rarely involves foretelling; rather, most often prophecy is a "telling forth" of what Jesus Christ communicates through the Spirit of Truth to a specific people, gathered in a place, at a time. St. Paul exhorted the primitive Church to "not quench the Spirit. Do not despise prophetic utterances. Test everything; retain what is good".

### Church's Stand on the Occult

Today there is a tremendous fascination with the mysterious and the unknown. The great scholar C. S. Lewis wrote, "There are two equal and opposite errors into which our race can fall about the devils. One is to disbelieve in their existence. The other is to believe, and to feel an excessive and unhealthy interest in them. They themselves are equally pleased by both errors and hail a materialist or a magician with the same delight." The modern age is strong proof of this unhealthy fascination. People are attracted to evil and captivated by it. They are vulnerable to temptation because of a growing revolt against science and technology that, for all their efforts, cannot meet man's spiritual hunger. If science and technology are supposed to produce all the good things, why haven't they accomplished it? Instead, there is a continuous degradation of personality. People are not treated as human beings anymore but as computer data, numbers assigned from womb to tomb. Today, a terrible spiritual vacuum exists in which people are forced to live because they turned away from God and tried to fill the resulting emptiness with physical pleasures and comfort using modern technologies. Today, the kingdom of the occult encompasses the globe like a spiderweb of immense proportions, its overall membership estimated in the hundreds of millions.

The occult seduces the unwary with its offer of limited knowledge of the future and supposed control over the lives of others. It promises power. If diviners can provide secret information to an individual that only they know, and then predict something that does indeed occur, then the diviners have secured power over the other person through fear. The occult holds out the promise of love, but it is not the divine, unconditional love of God as described in Scripture. Rather, it is psychosexual love, which explains why many of those who are in the world of the occult are immoral, recognizing only a standard of authority established by their own reasoning. The occult offers a small degree of certainty in a world of uncertainty. Moving outside the realm of established religion, it promises things that the Church forbids. It provides a sense of belonging, so desperately needed by people who reject God's love. At its heart it is egocentric: the occultist seeks first his own ends and then the ends of others. It provides no exit from the realities of life and the problem of sin. Whether it is spell-casting, tarot, astrology, trance, séance, mediumship or herbalism, these traditions offer tangible ways for people to enact change in their lives. For a generation that grew up in a world of big industry, environmental destruction, large and oppressive governments, and toxic social structures, all of which seem too big to change, this can be incredibly attractive.

We have seen the condemnation of the occult in the book of Deuteronomy to learn that God considered Canaanite occult practices "abominations" worthy of capital punishment. In these verses, God has given an index of occult practices. The world of the occult is to be avoided by believers in Christ because we are the temples of the Holy Spirit. So, the catholic church does not accept the occult practices.

## *The Spiritual Dimension of the Christian Life*

"The devout Christian of the future will either be a 'mystic,' one who has experienced 'something,' or he will cease to be anything at all.[2]" The experience of God is not something unusual; rather, to be human is to be open to the possibility of God's self-communication. This openness to Mystery as the horizon that is always ever greater is the possibility for the receipt of grace, which is defined as the communication of God's own self.

The discussion of spirituality is complicated by the fact that people often have different understanding of the concept. Wuthnow cites a study done by Conrad Cherry, director of the Center for the Study of Religion and American Culture at Indiana University, where 8% of respondents regard spirituality as contact with a supernatural world, 5% call it a way of life, 11% consider it as something about their own convictions and practices, 46% call it a system of beliefs or doctrines, 2% take it as a system of morality, 16% don't know what it means, and

7% believe it has no meaning. On the popular level spirituality is more likely to be taken as personal convictions in contrast to religion, which is more likely to be related to churches or organizations.

Spirituality may include a belief in a supernatural realm, personal growth, a quest for an ultimate or sacred meaning, religious experience, or an encounter with one's own inner dimension. The meaning of spirituality has developed and expanded over time, and various connotations can be found alongside each other. The term "spirituality" originally developed within early Christianity, referring to a life oriented toward the Holy Spirit. During late medieval times the meaning broadened to include mental aspects of life, while in modern times the term both spread to other religious traditions and broadened to refer to a wider range of experience, including a range of esoteric traditions. Fiona Gardener defined "Spirituality is that which gives life meaning that includes a sense of something beyond or greater than the self." One characteristic of spirituality is a balance between a purely intellectual or cerebral approach and a purely interiorized approach. The former engages the mind and nothing else. If we are just interested in the study of theology and do not pay attention to how it can affect our wills, our imaginations, our feelings, or if we are not interested in how it may have a bearing on the miraculous then we end up being dry and arid. On the other hand, a purely interiorized approach is interested in the mystical to the extent that it has very little to do with the realities of practical living in this world. Spirituality represents the interface between ideas and life, between Christian theology and human existence.

Spirituality is the experiential realisation of a transcendent reality. It refers to a relationship with a reality that reaches beyond the ego. The second aspect is about its experiential manifestation, i.e. a holistic type of knowing that includes cognition, affect and motivation.

What we are seeing in this mushrooming of spiritualities is a widespread ferment, a new awakening to the spirituality. If we were to survey the contemporary scene today, we would notice a renewed interest in traditional spiritual paths together with an almost bewildering variety of new developments. These developments can be roughly sorted into the following four groups:

1) Centering prayer and the work of Thomas Merton, the charismatic movement, fresh approaches to Carmelite, Benedictine, and Ignatian spirituality, the revival of spiritual direction, etc.;

2) Dream work, active imagination, focus on mid-life transitions, use of the Myers-Briggs Type Indicator, the Enneagram, journaling, the Twelve Steps, etc.;

3) Zen-Christian dialogue, Moslem-Christian dialogue, Hindu-Christian dialogue, and amalgamation of some of their practices with the Christian practices, etc.; and

4) Creation spirituality, Christian ecology movement, the new cosmologies, Native American spiritualities, the simple monastic movement, spiritualities derived from the peace and justice movements and liberation theology, etc.

A new awareness of the earth is beginning to enter Christian spirituality. One aspect of this development is the increasing utilization of the new cosmologies that have been one of the finest creations of modern physics. What could be the problem here, we might ask, in making use of the hard-won insights of modern science, from quantum mechanics to cosmic strings? These theories are certainly fascinating and stimulating and deserve our careful attention. The results are physico-mathematical constructs of undeniable operative power and efficacy, but these concepts do not aim at a point-to-point correspondence with reality, still less an explanation of the inner nature of things. It is going to be an extremely delicate job to penetrate the hypotheses of the physicist and discern their ontological and theological implications. If we erect a spirituality directly upon these physical theories, it is liable to have no more permanence than many of these theories themselves. The actual road stretching from the new cosmologies to Christian spirituality is much more difficult.

Our world today is engulfed in kind of spiritual schizophrenia, based on a dualistic set of perceptions whereby we divide reality into the opposing categories of God versus human, spirit versus matter, the sacred versus the secular. This in fact, is a deconstruction of our God-given reality; a way of thinking and behaving that undermines the spiritual and cultural wholeness of life. And there is a great deal of evidence to suggest that religion itself contributes significantly to this dilemma.

## The Need for Discernment between Charisms and the Occult

The charism of discernment of spirits is the empowerment to distinguish one spirit from another. The Baptized are called to conform their lives to God and to be transformed, as individuals and as Church, into His way and likeness. Discernment is required regarding the charisms themselves; this gift of discernment is proper to the office of the pastors of the Church.

We should not be seeking after supernatural signs and wonders for their own sake. Jesus warned us that false signs and wonders would characterize the end times. Paul tells us that the church is the pillar and foundation of truth. It is to be the setting where God's people are held accountable to the word and the truth it espouses. It is to be an environment where supernatural things are welcome, but all things are tested in the gatherings of the saints.

The Christianity of the Bible is a religion that is uncompromisingly supernatural. If we take away the supernatural, we take away Christianity. At the heart of the worldview of both Testaments is the idea that the realm of nature is created by one who transcends that nature. That God Himself is "supra" or above and beyond the created universe. The first principle of the Bible is that God must never be identified with the realm of nature but always and everywhere be the Lord over nature. The difference between the natural and the supernatural is the difference between that which is restricted to this world and that which participates in the realm of the divine, the realm that is above and beyond the reach of what is found in simple nature.

In no way does this affirmation of supernatural in the Bible belittle the importance of the natural. The natural realm is where God's work of redemption is played out in space and time. But that work of redemption is not a natural process of human evolution or development; rather, it involves an intrusion from above, from the transcendent realm of God, which addresses the spiritual nature of our humanity.

With the renewed interest in the supernatural that comes with the occult, we must be ever vigilant to make sure that whatever understanding we have of the supernatural is an understanding that is informed by the Bible. What we need is an understanding of the supernatural that comes to us from God so that our understanding of angels, or demons, or of spiritual beings comes from God's self-revelation and not from human speculation, neo-gnostic magic, or other forms of pagan intrusions. Again, we must insist that without the supernatural, Christianity loses its very heart, and this writer cannot understand why anybody would attach any great significance to Christianity at all once it's been stripped of its supernatural elements.

In this context, discernment is both possible and necessary to find out what is leading to life and what is leading to destruction. Many of the occult practices lead us to destruction and their promises are empty. It implies that we have both the ability and the space to exercise genuine freedom in decisions that touch upon the shape and direction of our lives as Christians regarding genuine Charisms and the occult practices.

"Do not conform any longer to the pattern of this world but be transformed by the renewing of your mind. Then you will be able to test and approve what God's will is – his good, pleasing, and perfect will". Discernment may be defined as a conscious experience of God's grace drawing one to a course of action. The development of the art of discernment is necessary because, if there are choices to be made, we need to have a process which enables us to make them well, under the leadership of the Spirit of God. God is constantly placing options before us. "I have set before you life and death, the blessing and the curse. Choose life, then, that you and your descendants may live, by loving the Lord your God[3]". Discernment is an integral part of every Christian's life-call, of every life of faith.

Periodically, we are challenged to take stock of our lives and make changes and adjustments in our choice of work, relationships and schedules. These times of transition can be unsettling, and they can be stressful as one begins to let go of the security of the familiar and searches for new clarity and direction. However, these periods also can generate new possibilities and a renewed sense of responsibility for one's life.

Testing the spirits, to use St. John's words, means to seek congruence between various impulses and possible options on the one hand, and this basic orientation of our lives on the other. Sifting and resting our inner experience, then requires a true desire to find God's kingdom within and enough spiritual freedom to allow that kingdom to rule our hearts. Aside from an awareness of this basic orientation and direction, discernment further demands a growing perceptiveness and sensitivity to what is going on in and around us- insights and memories, events and circumstances, feelings and tendencies.

## Endnotes

[1] Bultmann R., Kerygma and Myth, Harper & Row, New York, 1962, p.4

[2] Karl Rahner, "Christian Living Formerly and Today," in *Theological Investigations VII*, trans. David Bourke, NewYork, Herder and Herder, 1971, p.15

[3] Dt 30:19